ACE CARROWAY
AND THE
HANDSOME DEVIL

GUY WORTHEY

ACE CARROWAY AND THE HANDSOME DEVIL

Cover design: Brian Gagnon
Art: Mikey Brooks

ISBN: 1-949827-03-8
ISBN-13: 978-1-949827-03-3

WESTING PRESS

To Charlotte.

This above all: to thine own self be true,
And it must follow, as the night the day,
Thou canst not then be false to any man.

— William Shakespeare

To-night's Weather—FAIR

"10 TO 3"
DAILY WALL STREET
FEATURE THIS EDITION

The Evening World

"Circulation Books Open to All!"

Copyright, 1921, by The Press Publishing Co. (The New York World.)

NEW YORK, THURSDAY, SEPTEMBER 15, 1921

To-morrow's Weather—FAIR

WALL STREET
FINAL
EDITION

Entered as Second Class Matter, Post Office, New York, N. Y.

PRICE THREE CENTS

VOL. LXII NO. 21,846—DAILY

"Circulation Books Open to All!"

BABE RUTH BREAKS HIS OWN HOME RUN MARK WITH 55

DE VALERA TELLS BRITAIN "CONSENT OF THE GOVERNED" MUST BE BASIS OF PARLEY

Ireland Can Negotiate Only as a Sovereign State, Is Sinn Fein Reply to Lloyd George's Invitation.

Note Expresses Willingness to Confer at Inverness, but Points Out Erin Already Has Declared Independence.

Premier's Own Statement in 1918 Cited in Support of Irish Position—Envoys Now Are Being Chosen

RUTH GETS 55TH HOMER, SETTING A NEW RECORD

Beats His Mark of Last Year, a World One, in To-day's Game.

3 BLOCKS BURNED IN $350,000 FIRE AT ROCKAWAY BEACH

Believed Cause of Blaze— One Man Is Killed

FANNED BY HIGH WIND, BEACH CITY OFFICIALS

Fire Alarm Bring Engines From Brooklyn and All Nearby Resorts.

CITY PAYING ARMY FOOD SALE CLAIMS OF 300 WOMEN

Three Will Get Sen,884 Wish Lyons Office Salesworked Have Put in Demand.

OF $800,000 Surplus. All but $125,851 Has Gone for Charity.

ARBUCKLE TO KNOW TO-DAY WHETHER HE IS TO BE TRIED FOR MURDER OF MISS RAPPE

PARIS SEES EVILS OF PROHIBITION IN ARBUCKLE CASE

With Two Charges Against Comedian, Prosecutor Will Decide Which to Press—Release on Bail Asked.

Many Famous Movie Stars to Be Drawn Into Case as Witnesses to Tell of Actor's Alleged Orgies.

Girl Witnesses Back Up Story of "Fatty's" Accused—Arrangements Made for Miss Rappe's Funeral.

PERFORMING ARTS HAPPENINGS

SYMPHONY, OPERA, AND BROADWAY HIGHLIGHTS

Symphony's Second Concert of the Season
Saturday, September 17, 8 p.m.
Under the baton of Herr Oldman
Liszt "Les Preludes," Sibelius "Symphony No. 2," & Chopin "2nd Piano Concerto"
Cecilia Conway, pianist

Metropolitan Opera House – Reviews All Week	
Friday	Debut: Grace Bradlin, Suzanne Keenei, & Grace Anthony .... Lohengrin
Saturday	Debut: Mario Jeritza and George Meader .... Lucia di Lammermoor
Sunday	Debut: Amelita Galli-Curci .... In Trovitara

Up and Down the Great White Way

Shubert Theatre	Erminie and Gallina .... Eva LeGallienne in Liliom
Apollo Theatre	.... Lady Be Good
Little Theatre	The Taming of the Shrew (Next week, Hamlet)
Eltinge Theatre	.... The Importance of Being Earnest
Colonial Theatre	.... Marilyn Miller and Eddie Cantor in Sally
New Amsterdam Theatre	.... Little Johnny Jones
Broadhurst Theatre	.... Naughty Marietta
Olympic Theatre	.... The Red Mill
Princess Theatre	.... Ziegfeld's Revue
The New Theatre	.... Yip Yip Yaphank
Lyceum Theatre	.... La Belle Paree

[Continued in following columns]

PART ONE

THE MARK
OF THE
SNOW LEOPARD

Chapter 1

Hubert Ewing Devery Bostock III, more commonly referred to as Bert, pounded up the stairs to the upper floor of his Beacon Hill apartment. He entered the sitting room and spread his hands apologetically. "Sorry about that, Suzanne! Whoever rang the doorbell ran off. Nobody there, after all. Now, where were we?"

Strains of Benny Goodman exuded from the Radio-Victor machine. The redhead on the divan recrossed her legs. "Maybe the lightning scared them off. You were about to pour me some wine, I think."

"Was I? What a smart fellow I must be. That's a wicked wonderful idea."

Thunder rumbled, rattling the window panes.

Suzanne hugged herself. "It's shaping up to be a frightful night!"

"Only outside," said Bert. "Inside, it's cozy and warm." The phone rang before he could uncork the wine bottle.

"Suzanne, darling? Could you get that?"

Suzanne picked up the receiver. "Hello?" Her brows knitted. "What? Who's this?"

She turned to Bert to ask a question. Lightning flashed outside. The electric lights went dark without so much as a flicker. Suzanne gasped, "Oh, my!"

"Hold on! I have matches. Here." A match flared to life, illuminating the young lawyer's face.

He applied the match to a triple candelabra as Suzanne said, "Hello? Hello?" into the phone.

She slowly replaced the handset into its cradle and glanced at her handsome date. She arched an eyebrow. "It was a woman. She said she needed to see you. *Alone.*"

Bert assumed an air of innocence and splashed wine into two glasses. "A client, probably."

"A client. You'd better hope." They arranged themselves on the divan at the window and clinked glasses. They exchanged amused half-smiles in the candlelight. If it weren't inky black outside, there would be a view of Boston Common.

Lightning flashed again.

Suzanne's eyes flicked to the window and widened in horror. From her throat ripped an involuntary scream of pure terror. Bert whipped his head to look. He caught a glimpse only, lit by the last dim flicker of lightning. The eerie light outlined a shape hovering outside the second floor window. A hand splayed on the window. A face hovered beyond with dark hollows for eyes.

Bert's jaw dropped open. "A banshee!" Suzanne's voice shook. "A banshee! Scars on her face!"

He took a candle and raised it to the window. In the blackness nothing could be seen.

Suzanne broke the strained silence. "I want to go home."

Bert shook himself. "Yes. Yes, of course, Suzanne."

Roaring along in his two-seater roadster, she hesitantly narrated her impressions. A female form floated weightless and colorless in the lightning-light. Parallel lines of scars marred her cheek and temple. One hand extended toward the couple like a claw, or the soul-reaping scythe of an Irish banshee, the female spirit whose appearance heralded death.

His own fleeting impression he did not speak of. It was worse, more personal, and insane. But a woman who had died in a plane crash three months ago could not be floating outside his apartment window. His skin prickled.

By the time the young lawyer got back to his apartment, the lightning and thunder had ebbed, giving way to torrential rain. Bert set the brake on his car and bolted for the door to his apartment. He fumbled for his keys, but the unlocked knob turned under his hand. The door creaked open. Bert stared.

"Steady, Bert," he whispered, "A ghost wouldn't bother to jimmy the lock."

He crept in. The electric lights had come back on. There was a light upstairs. The Radio-Victor was playing, but not the Benny Goodman Bert had put on for Suzanne. It was Tommy Dorsey. Even as the eerie realization tightened his throat, an eager light ignited in his eye. Adventure was afoot.

Bert snaked a hand into the coat closet. His reaching fingers encountered a clammy, dripping wet raincoat. He suppressed a shout of panic. Breathing faster, he pushed his hand to the back right corner, where he kept his fencing epée. He felt its metallic hilt with a sense of relief. He advanced up the stairs, epée-point first.

His sword tip crossed the threshold of the sitting room.

"Who's there?" Bert said. "I'm warning you: I'm armed!"

A shadow across the room changed shape. A low trilling sounded; a haunting, musical warble that seemed to come from all corners of the room at once. The shadow glided forward into the light.

Bert's epée fell from suddenly-nerveless fingers with a clatter.

Chapter 2

A dry wind swept waves of flexing grass across the prairie hills. A sturdy fence followed each hilly undulation while marching in a geometrically perfect east-west line. A bay mare stood tethered to the fence, patient and motionless. Her eyes drooped sleepily and her lips sprouted a tuft of grass she had forgotten about mid-chew. Loops of coaxial, radio-frequency transmission cable protruded from her saddlebags.

Next to the animal, radio engineer Gregory Jamison knelt, weather-beaten face shaded by his Stetson. He briefly squinted at a dark dot low in the cerulean sky, then went back to trimming wire.

The mare's ear flicked. She raised her head and nickered as the sky-dot grew larger and buzzed like an oversized bee. Jamison, known to most by the nickname Tombstone, assured the horse, "It's jes' a plane, Sparky. Mebbe some joy-rider. Don't you worry none."

But once Tombstone had his cable strung, stapled, and connected, he looked again at the approaching airplane and frowned. All of a sudden it was loud, huge, and swift. It dived directly at him. Or so it seemed for a moment. The plane barrel-rolled as it passed the horse and man, the buzz of its engine fading rapidly.

Sparky neighed. Tombstone shook his fist at the departing plane. "Pesky whippersnapper! Come pester me in person, why don'tcha?"

A swish-thud sound interrupted Tombstone's tirade. He pivoted on his boot heel to the spot on the ground where his ears told him something heavy had landed. With a few ambling, slightly bowlegged steps, the lean cowboy strode over. He bent and picked up a sturdy soda bottle that hadn't been there a second ago.

Its smooth surface was marked with a black grease pencil. The lettering read, "Come to house." Under the letters was a stemmed heart symbol like the spade on a deck of cards.

Tombstone glanced back at the receding plane. It performed an effortless loop, then banked hard to the south, where his sister's ranch house lay.

"Tarnation." Tombstone pushed up the front of his hat to rub at a perplexed forehead.

Chapter 3

The rugby field in North Shields upon Tyne had rather gone to mud. Instead of putting a damper on the game, however, the deteriorating condition of the playing surface increased the enthusiasm of both crowd and competitors. A short, stout gentleman timidly rounded the bleachers. The stranger stroked at his new mustache. It was trimmed, waxed, and spiral curled at the ends. Among the arm-waving, fist-pumping people on the bleachers he saw only one umbrella; his own. He plucked a pocket-watch from his waistcoat. After reading the time, he clucked his tongue.

A sound like a pack of grizzly bears fighting over a carcass startled the mustachioed gent. He looked toward the playing field in alarm. A pile of struggling mud monsters swirled in a clump, snarling and bellowing. Upon second glance, they appeared to be men covered in field muck. Only hints of underlying jersey colors could be seen.

The clump of bodies pulsed, then burst outward. A red-haired, neckless brute emerged, victoriously hugging a large, oblong ball in his bulging arms. The atavism hurled the ball at a more average fellow standing nearby, who wore blue under his mud. The fellow seemed glad to catch it, though he was staggered by the force of the throw. He took off at a run, kicking up splashes of brown water at every step.

"Run, Lonnie!" shouted the red-haired muscleman.

But the slippery mud compromised Lonnie's ability to turn a corner and he skidded into another player whose jersey was red. There was a meaty splat, and the large ball squirted free. It arced through the air, and into the hands of another red-jerseyed player, who looked as astonished as anybody at the gift. But this chap had the legs of a stork, and he put them to use. Pursued by the entire mass of players, regardless of jersey color, he led the way down the length of the field. Inexplicably to the stranger, after all that effort, the stork-legged fellow belly flopped onto the mud behind the goalposts.

A man on the field wearing a jacket with vertical stripes blew on a whistle and called, "'At's the ga-ame!"

The blue-jerseyed players stopped running and their shoulders slumped in dejection. The red-jerseyed players kept running, surrounding the stork-legged fellow and whooping. Boos, cheers, applause, and indecipherable bawled syllables erupted from the soggy bleachers.

The mustachioed gent with the umbrella scanned the players. His name was Sam Raia Biming, an Egyptian-Chinese archaeologist currently attached to London's British Museum. He weaved around players smeared with brown coming off the field, each taller than himself. He honed in on the red-haired player with the massive chest and muscle bound arms and placed himself in the brute's path. The mud-covered centre also sported a mustache; a thick double waterfall of ginger. The centre halted as he discovered the dark gentleman in his path. His eyes grew round and his broad face grew incredulous. A few fellow players glanced over, wondering if the gentleman under the umbrella was about to get pulped.

But the red-haired fellow broke into a wide grin, and bellowed, "Blimey! If it hain't Sam! It is you, Sam?"

The short, rotund fellow enunciated like a walking dictionary. "It is I, Gooper. How are you, sahib? It has been long and long."

"Hoy! I dare say I'm healthy an' hale! What brings you to the match? A sudden interest in rugby? Interesting variant, rugby sevens. Very popular. I'd shake yer 'and but I know I'm a mess!" Gooper's grin did not fade as his cockney accents rolled.

Sam glanced left and right, then leaned forward. He spoke in hushed tones. "I am late because you are not at your university, sahib! You are here, playing this rugby football contest. Gooper, we must travel. We must go to America, and soon. The ship departs Liverpool tomorrow!"

"Wot? Naw, naw. Oi've got ter get back ter Wales. No time ter go galavantin' across the pond!" Gooper's given name was Phileas Locknard. He was a field biologist, loosely connected to the University of Cardiff.

"Shh! Not so loud! You will want to, sahib. I have had telegrams. Sensitive telegrams. The last one was in code!"

Gooper's brow furrowed. "Go on. Wot did they say?"

Sam shook his head from side to side emphatically. "I will not say it out loud. I will show you." He tucked his umbrella under his arm and fished a folded paper scrap from a waistcoat pocket. He unfolded it and shielded it with his hands so that no one but Gooper could see. It was silly, of course. No one at the rugby tournament paid them the slightest attention, now that no one was being pummeled.

Gooper squinted at the telegram. Underneath typed gibberish Sam had penciled his deciphered transcription. Gooper's jaw grew slack.

"This is true?"

"Yes, sahib."

"Oi'll pack me bags."

CHAPTER 4

Drizzle dampened the gloom of late night on Broadway. The door under the "Stage Entrance" sign opened, and a couple stepped out into the Londonesque New York alley. The lamp over the lintel illuminated their faces for a moment. Both were handsome and dressed in overcoats, the man blonde, the woman brunette.

"That was rough," remarked the man. "I wish the costumes were finished. It would help set the mood."

"Speak for yourself, Warburton," the woman said lightly. "You don't have to deal with whalebone corsets and ten stones of skirt layers."

"True enough! But the symbolism of a heavy costume built of prison-like bars is particularly apt for Ophelia's character. Poor Ophelia."

"Yes, she's a tragic character. Not that Prince Hamlet survives the play, either, of course. Oh! What was that? A rat? It sounded bigger than a rat."

The man glanced behind them into the alley gloom. A garbage barrel rocked in tightening circles, settling back to rest. Man and woman regarded the scene for a few moments, but nothing further sounded. Nothing further moved.

"Just our fan club, apparently," quipped Warburton. Boxnard Warburton Snana also responded to the nickname Quack, though there was nothing duck-like about his motions or manners. "Let's press on. Still up for a nightcap?"

"Yes. Let's go."

They strolled onto Broadway itself, then down a half block. They slipped into a wine bar, still somewhat crowded despite the late hour. A bearded customer with a rolling basso voice greeted them. "Hamlet and Ophelia? You're late! And also, you are together. Anything going on I should know about?"

Quack pursed his lips at the bearded fellow, cast as Claudius in the play. His answer was curt. "Yes. We'd like a drink."

"Two clarets, please," the actress told the bartender. She pulled Quack down to the nearest table for two, effectively cutting off further conversation with Claudius.

"Don't let him get under your skin," she said in low tones.

"He's irritating. How do you stay so calm?"

"You get used to it."

"It's gender, isn't it?" Quack mused. "An actress has to develop defenses against loose talk, and quick. Quicker than an actor."

Unnoticed, a figure in an overcoat — collar high, hat pulled low — drifted in from the back. The apparition slipped into an empty table in the darkest corner and did not remove the hat.

Minutes passed. Conversations swirled like minnows in an eddy around the dimly lit bar. The actress left Quack to visit the powder room.

The shadowy figure moved, slipping forward toward the seated blond actor.

Quack noticed something at his left elbow. He glanced at it. A playing card? He swiveled left, then right, quick and alert. An overcoated shadow disappeared out the front. His knees flexed, as if desiring action, but he kept to his seat and examined the card. It was an ordinary ace of spades.

He held it by the candle to read tiny, neatly handwritten lettering. "Ditch her. We need to talk."

Quack stared at the card, then looked wildly around. The server set two wine glasses down. "Sorry, sir. Didn't mean to startle you."

"Ah, not a worry, friend," Quack said, his voice none too steady.

"Wine is served? Good timing!" the actress said, slipping into her seat. As she examined Quack she lost her smile. "You look pale."

"Indeed, I feel a bit pale. Do you mind if I, erm, ditch you? Here." Quack dug out his wallet and dropped a dollar onto the table as he rose to his feet.

"Oh, not at all! Take care of yourself, Boxnard."

Quack rushed to the door and out onto Broadway. In one of the countless cones of light that dotted the street, an overcoat and hat leaned. His pace slowed as if he had run over a patch of glue. Quack approached the shadowed figure with caution and a growing sense of unreality. Twin glints of gold under the hat brim shadow marked eyes that watched his every move.

Quack decelerated even more as he neared. His jaw grew slack. His voice came out hoarse. "Am I seeing a ghost?"

CHAPTER 5

"'Yes' might be the answer closest to the truth," replied the shadowy apparition with a wry curve of her lips. Only the lower parts of her face caught enough street light to be seen. "Apologies for breaking up your date, Quack. You and Bert both."

"Never mind about that! She's a career girl, too focused to get tangled up in a romance. As for Bert, he deserves it. But, Ace! It's really you? You're not dead! What happened?"

"Quack, come on. We're going to the Tilesbrink Hotel. I'll tell all, there." The overcoated figure reached for the actor's upper arm and steered him uptown.

He stumbled along unresisting for several paces, then stopped in his tracks and broke into a bright grin. "You're not dead!"

Ace returned to him and pushed him gently, laughing softly. "Your instincts are always to be trusted, Quack. I'll trust you on that point in particular."

Quack walked briskly now, matching the tall woman stride for stride. "Why are we going to a hotel?"

"I gathered us all, the *Flugzeugfabrik*[1] six. The rest await us at the hotel. You're the last to know. Apologies for the last-minute abduction, but you were the

---

[1] Airplane factory. German language.

easiest to locate. Your name's on the marquee."

Quack whistled in wonderment. "Wind and stars! The whole gang?"

Minutes later, they padded across carpeted hotel floors to a door labeled "Meeting Room." A stout man just outside the door appeared at first glance to be hotel staff, crisply dressed in a suit with a European cut. But the door warden beamed with pleasure when he spotted the approaching pair. His black mustache, carefully waxed, spiraled artfully at the ends.

Quack exclaimed, "Sam!" and seized the shorter man's hand in both of his to pump up and down. "I like your mustache, but I almost didn't know you."

"Sahib. My heart grows wings and flies." Sam shook hands back, then exchanged a handshake with Ace.

"Are the others, here?" Quack said.

"Mm, hm. Listen." Ace's hat nodded toward the closed door.

Faint through the door, a Cockney baritone emerged. "I'm preferrin' 'sesquipedalian,' eh? Wot d'ye think?"

A drawl from the American west replied, "How 'bout 'loquaciously ostentatious?'"

The Cockney admitted, "It's got some merit, 'ceptin it's two words an' not one."

"Ah, yep. How 'bout good ol' 'polysyllabic,' then?"

"That'll do nicely."

"Hot diggety! So we're agreed. Yer a polysyllabic pinniped."

"Yeh, a walrus wot likes big words, that approximates the centrality of— Hey! Are you insultin' me, lizard man?"

The listeners at the door exchanged nostalgic smiles. Ace said, "We should go in before it comes to blows."

Sam opened the door and they filed into the wood-paneled room. Bert slumped in one of six chairs set around a table, massaging his temples. He perked up as Ace, Sam, and Quack filed in. Gangly Tombstone's western style shirt and denim pants hung loosely on his bony frame. Tombstone stood facing broad Gooper, whose bulging chest threatened to burst buttons on a tweed vest and coat.

Bert unslumped and proclaimed, "We're all here. Wicked good."

Quack forged forward to clasp hands and pound backs. "Tombstone! Gooper! Good to see you!" The actor looked sidelong at Bert. "But who invited the shyster?"

"Glad to see you, too, Quack. So glad they never let you practice medicine." Bert and Quack stared cooly at each other; two trim, handsome figures about the same height. Bert's dark hair and gray eyes contrasted with Quack's blond waves and blue hazel irises.

Quack gave a contemptuous sniff and asked, "How is it we are all gathered right here, right now? Did Ace arrange it?"

"Yes, that's right," Ace said. Her back was turned. She wedged a chair under the meeting room doorknob; a crude lock.

Bert said, "I was on a date with the most eligible bachelorette in Boston. Ace rang the doorbell, called on the telephone, and then accidentally spooked Suzanne. Spooked me, too, come to think of it."

"She sent me telegrams in code," Sam said. "I brought Gooper."

Tombstone said, "I was fixin' a decameter-wave antenna at m' sister's spread up in South Dakota. Ace flew by an' dropped a message."

Ace joined the group and shed her overcoat. She wore a flight suit underneath, with a wide belt. She took off her hat to reveal unkempt, short hair. As the shadows lifted from her face Quack gasped. Four parallel scars slashed diagonally across her temple and cheekbone. "What? Ace! What happened?"

Sam said, "She has not told us, sahib. She wished to wait until you, too, were here."

Ace shrugged her shoulders. "I'll try. I'm not sure I'll make a lot of sense, but I'll do my best. You'd all better sit."

CHAPTER 6

Ace sat, too, and scanned the circle of concerned expressions. To the men, she seemed much the same as during the war, except for the scars. She seemed to have grown another inch or two taller, and her face had lengthened. Her golden coloring and quick manner remained the same.

Still, it was eerie to see her again, solid and alive. Eerie and exciting at the same time, like hair standing on end at the approach of an electrical storm.

"Fellas. Glad to see your motley mugs again, after all this time. I have a proposition for you, but I'll get to that after I fill you in on my disappearance. The newspapers pronounced me dead, evidently."

"Yeah," Tombstone said, his long face sad-eyed as a basset hound.

"No explanation. Just missing and presumed dead in Tibet or China," Quack said.

Ace said, "The explanation is that Darko Dor hired a gang to hide a time bomb in my airplane. It detonated while I was over the Himalayas."

A confused babble broke out.

"Wot?"

"But he's dead!"

Ace held up her hand, palm out. The babble died down. "He survived the car crash at the *Flugzeugfabrik*. Like some of the Ottoman officers you read about from time to time, he went into hiding after the Great War. Now, he has resurfaced as an international criminal. Furthermore, he is responsible for my father's murder."

"No!" Quack said.

"Lemme at 'im!" Tombstone pounded a fist into an open palm.

Ace smirked at Tombstone. "Let's hash that out later. First, let me attempt to tell how I fared before I lose my nerve."

"Lady Ace. You have courage in plenty," Sam said.

"Well, we'll see, Sam. I may shortly come off as insane." Ace steepled her fingers and closed her eyes. "The bomb blew most of the tail off and started one wing on fire. I had control over the ailerons, but that was all. The Flyer spiraled downward. I managed to hit a snow field and not bare rock."

The memory of the frantic few moments replayed vividly in her mind. She fought for vision in the blast of icy air jetting through the space that moments ago were windows. She fought for control of the falling remnants of the airplane. She fought all the way to impact.

"That's all I knew, for a while. I blacked out."

Her eyes opened, but seemed focused on a scene beyond the mundane room they sat in. She continued, with pauses as she groped for words.

"I opened my eyes, though they were sticky with blood."

Nothingness gave way to a world composed of pain. Her senses came awake, but impressions from the real world fought through a towering wall of agony before leaking through to her consciousness.

"I lay half-buried on the snow slope in the wreckage of my Lockheed Flyer. The cockpit was mostly intact, but the remains of the tail lay in front of me, not behind."

A dim twilight of swirling snow hissed over dark crags and jagged boulders. Arctic winds moaned like lonely giants. Twisted metallic debris lay strewn over the snowfield. A few tattered metallic arcs caged her field of view like decaying ribs. She thought to herself, 'This is the landscape where death walks.'

"I could tell I was in a bad way. I felt numb. Disconnected from what was real. I wondered if I was alive or dead, and I truly could not decide which it was.

"It didn't help my confused thoughts when a giant cat emerged out of the swirl of snow."

Beyond the nearby metal, a vision of calm materialized. It padded toward the injured flyer, a snow leopard marked with vivid dark abstract designs. It paused in its glory of wild splendor and regarded Ace with steady gray eyes.

"We looked at each other. The creature seemed to me the only real thing in the universe. The scenery, my own body, the wreckage, it all seemed a million miles away. I slumped in my cockpit seat, sagging against the safety belts. The snow surface was at eye level.

"I blinked. Or maybe I blacked out again. The enormous cat was closer. A snow leopard."

A being silent and magical, to move without being seen to move.

"I whimpered, the tiny sound swallowed up in the primal icy air. I said, 'Go away.' Or perhaps I only dreamt that I spoke aloud.

"The large cat did not go. It padded forward. Its luminous eyes compelled and demanded. I twitched. The tiny movement caused pain that almost overwhelmed me.

"When the pain stars in my vision cleared, the cat's face loomed inches away."

Its visible breath puffed to caress her numb lips between howls of the mountain winds.

"Its eyes pulled at me in a way I can never describe. Its force pulled at something other than what exists in the physical world.

"But I shrank back from the spiritual tug. In defiance, I closed my eyes. I wanted defeat. I didn't care about life or death. I desired only peace and a release from the agony, even if that meant oblivion."

Ace fell silent. The five men gazed, rapt, as she struggled for words. A rueful half smile flitted across her face.

"The leopard batted me, claws out, raking me across temple and cheek."

Her eyes flew open. She screamed.

"The leopard calmly padded back a few paces. It glanced at me over its shoulder as I panted. I spoke aloud.

"'So help me, spirit! That was beyond insulting! You win. I am alive.'

"I forced numb hands to release the seat belt. Part of the fuselage had split and curled over. It sliced into my thigh, imprisoning me in my seat. I bent the duraluminum back with my hands, adding cuts on my thumbs to the gash on my thigh. Every clumsy movement lanced pins and needles through me, and yet I could barely feel cloth or metal or even the air of the real world."

The snow leopard alone remained clear in her vision.

"I told the leopard, 'I'm freezing to death, aren't I? I read about how it's a pleasant way to die. You go numb and you sleep.' I could taste my own blood on my tongue.

"I staggered free of the still-smoking wreckage. My poor Lockheed Flyer. I lurched after the snow leopard. No part of my body obeyed me very well.

"The cat blinked its gray eyes and seemed to smile. It moved on, then paused to wait. I struggled to follow, huffing for air. I fell, again and again."

With each fall, she left red spatter that moments later froze into crimson crystals in the snow.

"Over and over, I dragged myself back upright, and the snow leopard stayed within sight.

"In the lee of a cliff face, I saw ledges crudely hewn out of the rock. I stared stupidly at them for a long time before I realized they were shaped by human hands for human feet. The snow leopard smiled down on me from halfway up."

The snow leopard padded up the stairs and disappeared into a veil of windblown snow.

"I clawed my way up, inch by inch."

Her fingers slipped on freezing rock. Her clumsy feet scrabbled for insecure footholds. Time exploded to an infinite stretch of unending calamity.

"Eventually, I found that there was no next step. I crawled onto a flat place. I looked for my guide. The snow leopard had grown and darkened. It metamorphosed into a wooden rectangle with a triangle roof on top and a door in the middle. I dragged myself on.

"I had gone out of my head, or close to it. My precious intellect, the vanity of my life, so nurtured by my father, had shattered to pieces. All I knew was that I needed to move forward or die."

"Well." Ace lifted her chin. "I had decided not to die."

Chapter 7

Ace's eyes refocused. She blinked at the row of aghast facial expressions.

She laughed, then clapped a hand over her mouth to stifle it. Still wearing an impish grin, she said, "I'm sorry, fellas! I lived, honest. I'm not so sure about the snow leopard, but the wooden hut turned out to be real. I lurched through the door, and then I fell on my face for the last time. A couple of days later, I awoke with the scent of jasmine tea in my nostrils."

"Someone took care of you, Lady Ace?" said Sam.

"Yes. The hut belonged to a monk. As fate would have it, the same monk who gave up on me and sent me home a few months back. Rajanathan is his name."

"I suppose the feller didn't have a telephone," Tombstone said.

"Correct," said Ace. "And I wasn't up to travel for quite a while. I had several broken bones in my foot, and I hadn't done the injury any good by hiking on it in the Himalayas."

"Are you all right?" Quack said.

"Yes, Quack. I know how to set bones, though I must admit it was rather a trial to set my own, to say the least."

"Blimey!" Gooper said, huffing through his mustache. "Yew 'ealed up well, Ace. No limp. No 'obblin' around. Some scarrin' …"

Ace's hand twitched toward her face, then she shoved the appendage under the table. "As Raja put it, perhaps the snow leopard was not entirely a figment of my imagination." She cleared her throat. "As I healed in the mountain retreat, Raja and I discussed many things. The snow leopard, the death of my father, and the philosophy of revenge."

Bert leaned forward, intent. "Revenge? Is that why you got us together? We're going to hunt down Darko Dor?"

Ace shook her head. "No, not as such. We talked over why Darko Dor fixated on me. Why he tortured me with the death of my father, then attempted to kill me. Now, I fully agree we need to deflate Darko Dor one of these days. The reason I tried to be secretive in getting us all here tonight was so that Darko Dor would not discover that I'm alive. But, no, it's not about revenge."

"Then what, Lady Ace?" Sam said.

"I'm glad we're all together," Quack said. "I'm glad to see everybody. Even Brat."

Bert rolled his eyes ceilingward. "That's Bert, you oaf."

Ace spoke earnestly. "Think back to the Great War. We pulled together. We fought for the cause of freedom; something bigger than all of us. But after the war, we relaxed back into the grind of modern life. We all followed our separate interests and started careers. But let me ask you, does it not feel aimless in comparison to the higher purpose that united us in the war?"

"Does a bronco buck?" Tombstone said dolefully.

"Yes, those words ring true, Lady Ace," Sam said.

"In spades," Bert said.

"Absolutely," Quack added.

"Superlatively affirmative," Gooper said with a serene smile of mouth and mustache.

"Right. Since that is the case, I have a proposal. It involves considerable danger, and the odds are excellent that one or all of us will be killed."

Five pairs of eyes looked back at Ace for a while. The men exchanged uncertain glances. Eventually, Tombstone said, "That there's a point in favor already. What's the rest?"

Ace laughed. "And that's why I invited you all. You're wonderful. Crazy, but wonderful. Alright, here's the idea."

Ace sprang to her feet and paced. "I learned a few things from a detective in Hyannis, and I did a lot of thinking in Nepal. I decided that I want to fight crime."

"Oh!" Sam's eyebrows shot up. His mustache curls bounced.

Ace said, "There's a lot of organized crime these days. I'd like to open a detective agency here in New York."

"A detective agency," Quack murmured, tasting the words.

"Wicked interesting proposition," Bert said.

Ace nodded. "We'll take the hard cases. We'll chase crime bosses like Darko Dor. There are more like him out there. He's probably not even the worst of the lot. If we're successful, we'll make a lot of them angry. We'll all be targets from time to time."

Ace spread her hands in entreaty. "I'm saying 'we,'

because I want all of you as partners. You'll have to take breaks from your careers so you can come fight crime with me. I know it's a lot to ask." Ace scanned the row of faces, diverse in size, shape, color, and facial hair embellishment. "But I'm asking."

They spoke on top of each other.

"When do we start?"

"How much do you need to get going? I'll get my checkbook."

"May I purchase a set of brass knuckles? I have always wanted a set."

"Crikey! Count me in."

"Ah reckon Ah could swing a few years' time off."

Ace looked from face to face, her eyes going watery and her throat thickening. As the affirmations died down, she said, "Thank you. Truly. But there's one thing more. A thing a snow leopard taught me: No one is irredeemable, no matter how far down the path of foolishness or selfishness or evil they have gone. Even the most hardened criminal can awaken and build a better life. I know they don't often do. I'm not being unrealistic. But I want to make a point not to kill anyone intentionally. That's all. We might use guns now and then, but I don't want us aiming to kill, even when that might be more convenient. It is not our job to decide who lives and who dies. We shall always strive to preserve life. Are we agreed on this?"

Somberly, now, the five nodded assent.

"Yeh. 'Tis noble."

"We'll take the high road."

"Glad you said that, Ace! I'm with you!"

Ace's shoulders relaxed, releasing tension. She plopped down in her chair and grinned. "I feel so fabulous right now! All right, here's what's next." She rattled off, "Quack, you live in town. Find an office building in Manhattan with a floor we can rent and renovate. Bert, put an ad in the paper for a receptionist. They'll need to be a hard nut, but smart, too. Tombstone, we'll need custom lighting, microphones, tape recorders, chart recorders, and telephones. We need two-way radio communication with a car or two and hopefully a plane and a boat soon. Start pulling those materials together. Gooper and Sam, I want a hangar at the very nearest airport, and I want some slip space at the harbor. I'll work on filling those spaces."

"Fellas," concluded Ace, "No need to advertise that I'm alive just yet. It'll leak out, soon enough, but before the rats come swarming, I want to be armed with rat poison."

Part Two

C. Carroway
and
Associates

Chapter 8

Over the next few days, some infinitesimal fraction of New York's endless buzz of energy was diverted toward a nondescript four story office building at the intersection of Wall and Broadway. The new detective agency took up half of the third floor, the other half being a commercial photography studio. The agency secretly extended to the fourth story, which required significant alterations. Contractors and workmen re-made walls, re-plumbed pipes, and rewired the electricity. Ace directed most of the work. The lab ate up the most floor space, followed by the infirmary and library, and Tombstone was often busy in the communications room. Downstairs, a reception area and lounge presented the agency's public face, but an observation room would sit adjacent.

Bert ran an advertisement for a receptionist. He and Ace sat in a swirl of orderly chaos in the new office as workers smoothed plaster on walls and delivered furniture. A steady drizzle of candidates came for their appointments.

By the eleventh one, Bert was squirming in his seat. "Would any of them make adequate second choices, in case the perfect one doesn't come along?" Bert surreptitiously rubbed his sore rump.

Ace replied, "There's only one more to talk to, today. Let's see how it goes."

Bert forced a smile. "I see her coming in. I'll fetch her." He stood bent for a moment. With a groan, he straightened and went to escort the lady.

The last interviewee was a middle aged woman, upright and straight-laced, with a ribbon-trimmed hat several years out of fashion. A double row of buttons marched up the front of her high-collared dress. "Fiona Figgins," she sourly announced. She perched on the very edge of the chair offered by Bert and clutched the bag on her knees as if it were a medieval shield.

"Hubert Bostock, ma'am. This is Cecilia Carroway."

Bert sat back down, and Fiona Figgins handed a sheaf of papers to Ace. "My references," she said like a testy schoolmarm.

"Thank you, Mrs. Figgins. How many words can you type?" Ace studied Mrs. Figgins, then scanned through the documents.

"Sixty words per minute without errors."

"This is a detective agency. We'll probably get a lot of silly calls and calls for the sorts of jobs we don't take, like spying on spouses. So we're hoping you don't mind telling people 'no.' Do you enjoy telling salesmen to go away?" Ace fixed her eyes on Mrs. Figgins after her question.

Mrs. Figgins replied humorlessly. "Absolutely. Especially after they've given me free samples or cleaned half my floor."

Bert's eyes widened.

Ace said, "And dictation. Any problem keeping up if someone calls and rattles on for a while?"

"Not a problem. I use Pitman shorthand."

"Do you like small dogs?"

"The yippy ones? No. Can't abide them."

"Mornings might be slow. Do you have a hobby?"

"Well, I knit. And I like to work problems in probability and statistics."

"Any problem working for a female boss?"

"It'd be a breath of fresh air!" Mrs. Figgins said with animation. Belatedly, she looked at Bert and her mouth reluctantly stretched into an imitation of a smile.

"You're hired," Ace said. Bert appeared as if he had just swallowed a marble.

Ace said, "Standard pay for two weeks, then a permanent twenty five percent raise. Holidays off, plus ten more days a year. This being a detective agency, we might get a few irate individuals. If you ever feel that you are in personal danger, we'll have hidden switches that summon help. If all that sounds good, then ..." Ace trailed off and zeroed in on Bert. "We didn't draw up a contract yet, did we?"

Bert winced. "No, ma'am."

"Well, if all that is acceptable, Mrs. Figgins, Mr. Bostock here, who is a Legum Magister, will handdraft you a contract on the spot." The corners of Ace's mouth twitched in suppressed laughter.

"Thirty percent raise after the two weeks."

"Done."

Later, Bert asked Ace, "Did you hire Mrs. Figgins because she said she likes probability and statistics or because she said she likes a female boss?"

Ace said, "Neither, though I approve of both of those things. No, at the very beginning, she handed me her references. The other candidates handed theirs to you. It was a small thing, but it told me she was observant of subtleties."

"Ah, I see. Oh, well. So be it." Bert was detectably downcast over the decision. Then again, he had shown a certain bias against all candidates who hadn't had pretty ankles.

Chapter 9

Later that day, Ace weaved through crowded New York sidewalks. As she scouted for a café, a tiny sign caught her eye, half hidden behind a tree and bicycles propped against a metal railing. It said "Low Dive Café" with an arrow pointing down some stairs to the basement of a tenement.

The name sounded aeronautical. It drew her like a magnet. She sauntered over and descended worn stairs. She pushed through a battered door into a zone of pleasant smell. The windowless, shabby space felt comfortable and lived-in. Six small tables made a ragged semicircle around a counter equipped with stools. A few patrons sat drinking coffee or slurping soup.

Conserving energy behind the counter was a hill of a man. His elephantine arms rested crossed over an impressive paunch. One bicep bore a tattoo in the shape of a gray anchor with a faded red "MOM" printed across it. His fuzzy crew cut looked military, but creases of good humor crisscrossed his placid face.

"Gimme a Philly, Mom," said a lean freckled man on a stool.

"Comin' up, Fred," the tattooed giant replied in a thick Bronx accent. He spotted Ace coming in. "Sit wherever you want, miss."

Ace sat one stool down from Fred and studied a grease-splattered chalkboard wall menu whose age could likely be measured on a geologic time scale.

"What's the soup?" she asked.

"Chicken noodle," said Mom over his shoulder. Seemingly without conscious thought, he slapped a blob of lard on the hot griddle and added sliced green pepper and onion that immediately began to sizzle.

"Great. Give me that, and a coffee," Ace said.

"Call me Mom. Everybody does."

"All right, Mom. I'm Ace. Were you in the Navy?"

"Yeah, submarine fleet."

Fred, an angular man in a Macintosh, shifted his gaze from Ace's scars to Ace's eyes. "He was ship's cook."

A woman in factory coveralls with dark circles under her eyes dragged over to the counter. "Warm up my coffee, Mom?"

Mom turned the onions and green peppers with a spatula, then tonged some thin slices of beef to join the sizzling vegetables on the grill. He freed one hand to refill the factory worker's coffee, his eyes on the golden skinned flyer. Somehow, he didn't spill a drop. "Ace is a heckuva nickname. Your last name start with a 'C' by any chance?"

Her eyes sparked with a glint of alarm. Warily, she admitted, "Yeah."

Mom beamed, his eyes disappearing into a mass of smile wrinkles. "I gotcha. You're good folks, Ace. Make yourself at home. Soup and a cuppa Joe comin' … right about now." Mom's beefy hands slid a piping hot bowl of soup and a steaming mug of coffee in front of Ace.

Mom addressed the whole diner. "She's a fellow veteran, an' that means she's family."

Fred grinned and faux-whined, "Yes, Mother."

The sparse collection of people chuckled.

Ace felt a warmth inside from more than just the soup, and decided she liked the Low Dive Café.

After the Low Dive, Ace stopped at the hotel for a change of clothing. Worried that the foot she broke during the crash was not yet to full strength, she donned a pair of light shoes and knickers and headed back outside for a run. She whisked past the hotel doorman into the clement September night. The doorman watched the fleeting figure recede. He shook his head philosophically. "The guest is always right."

Ace's ghostly form crisscrossed Manhattan from the coarse banana dock district to swanky uptown. She monitored her foot more than she paid attention to the dwindling number of New Yorkers in the deepening gloom of night.

But one uptown gentleman caught her eye. He was tall, and walked with sure steps. He carried a box of Belmont chocolates from which a yellow gift tag dangled. His suave, virile face made Ace look twice. Under a prominent, straight brow, his quick gray eyes flicked toward the swiftly moving woman.

Ace ran past him in seconds, but the vision stayed with her, and a quizzical smile touched her lips. Her smile soon faded, and her hand raised to touch her scars. The echo of a woman's scream reverberated in her memory. The face of Bert's date through the window transformed into a rictus of horror and revulsion. Ace's jaw tightened. She ran on, alone

Twenty yards later, from the dark slot of an alley opening, Ace's keen ears caught a faint moan. It sounded human. It sounded like pain. Ace braked, and peered down the alley as the agonized glissando repeated. Barely in the gloom, she saw a feebly moving heap.

Ace sharply called toward the receding back of the chocolate-bearing man, "Sir! Call an ambulance! Someone is hurt!"

He turned in a hurry and called back, "Oh! Yes, ma'am! Right away!" She signaled thumbs-up and ducked into the inky alley.

The prone body resolved into a middle aged woman in suede shoes, tailored dress, and a mink stole. A purse lay near, amid a scatter of small items spilled from it.

Ace knelt by the delirious woman and examined what she could see of the lady in the gloom. A nasty lump swelled on the side of her head, and one of her fingers canted over at an unnatural, sideways angle.

For a moment, Ace debated over the broken finger. Before the woman regained full consciousness, Ace acted. With strong, knowing fingers, Ace tugged the woman's broken finger straight, then let the tension relax. The delicate splintered bones settled into place.

The woman moaned sharply. Her eyelids fluttered.

"Take your time, ma'am. I'm a doctor," Ace said. She patted herself for tools, but her usual wide belt languished back at the hotel. "I won't forget my tool belt again," she muttered. She searched elsewhere. Her own pocket held a handkerchief. She found a cosmetics paintbrush among the scattered contents of the victim's purse. Ace ripped strips of cloth from the bandana, using her teeth to get the rips started. She bound the paintbrush to two of the woman's fingers as a makeshift splint.

Ace looked up from her work and met haunted eyes. The woman gripped Ace's elbow with her uninjured hand.

"It was like a man, but with the face of a giant rat!" she said in strained tones. "It was horrible!"

Chapter 10

Some minutes later, the man with the box of chocolates arrived in the alley to a deceptively quiet scene. Ace sat on the dank cobblestones, using her thigh as a pillow for the woman's head. "I called," the man said. "What's going on? I didn't know what to tell them, but they said they would come anyway."

Ace replied, "She was struck unconscious. Her finger was broken, too." She looked down, "Keep your eyes closed, Mrs. Gemrock. It is best to stay as still as possible."

"I heard you the first time, Cecilia," the prone woman murmured in uptown accents.

"Oh!" the man said. He repositioned his box of chocolates behind his back and extended a hand to Ace. "Cecilia, is it? I'm Braggs. Jeremy Braggs."

Ace shook it. The man's grip was strong. She squeezed harder to match. "Thanks for calling the ambulance, Mr. Braggs. I'm Cecilia Carroway. This is Sarah Gemrock."

A siren wailed in the middle distance. Jeremy Braggs rubbed at his chiseled chin. "Cecilia Carroway. That rings a bell, somehow."

"Does it?" Ace said, "In that case, could you do me a favor? Another favor, I mean."

"But of course! Anything!" His enthusiasm was obvious. He stared fixedly at Ace's face.

"Please don't tell any reporters you met me," Ace

said glumly, "I'd like to avoid them."

"Oh, my! You're really Ace Carroway, the pilot? It's all coming back, now. You're supposed to be dead!"

"Yes, and I'm not quite ready to be alive again. So, mum's the word?" Ace tried putting on a smile.

To Ace's surprise, the smile seemed to have an effect. Braggs gushed, "Oh, mum's the word! Say no more! Oh, I can't believe this!"

"I hear the ambulance," said Mrs. Gemrock.

It came. The drivers gently bundled Mrs. Gemrock into the back, heeding advice by Ace. "Goodbye for now," Ace said, before they closed the doors.

After the ambulance pulled away, Ace felt eyes on her. A smiling Braggs stood almost at her elbow.

"Miss Carroway?"

"Yes?"

"Can I see you again?"

"Why?" Ace blurted. She drew herself stiff and tall. "Pardon. I don't mean to be rude. I've been away and I'm rusty on courtesy."

"I don't mind. I'll answer the same way, flat out. I find you very interesting. Very. Please, may I have your address? Or a phone number?"

"Ahem!" a new voice interrupted.

They swiveled to face the street. A rumpled trench coat stood there with an unshaven man inside it. The fellow slouched next to a black sedan, hands buried in his coat pockets. He regarded Ace and Braggs through sharp eyes. The end of a toothpick hung out the side of his mouth. "Dis where the mugging took place?" he said in gravelly tones.

"I found the victim ten yards down the alley." Ace

pointed to the spot.

"I didn't see anything. Who are you?" Braggs said.

"Call me Ironclad." He swiveled his toothpick to the other side of his mouth. "I beat the police, huh? Well, they're busy these days."

Ace studied the clean, black car. The light was dim, but the letters "U S GOVT" marched along under the larger numerals.

Braggs frowned. "What kind of name is Ironclad? Anyway, we were just leaving."

"Sure, sure. But it'll save time if you give me your names and addresses before you go. I'll pass it on to the authorities. Promise."

"You'll get no such thing from me, buster!" Braggs lifted his squared off chin defiantly.

Ace drifted toward the sidewalk. "You have an unconventional style, Mr. Ironclad, but I can deduce reasons to trust you. I'm Cecilia Carroway. 301 Wall, Suite 3A. Business hours, please."

The trench coat's occupant saluted Ace with his pencil stub. "Just Ironclad will do." He jotted notes in his notepad. Braggs spluttered indignantly. Ace did not stay to see how the pair fared.

The next day, the construction activity ebbed. Almost all the furniture was in. Mrs. Figgins unboxed a brand new typewriter. Ace stretched a tape measure across a window-like open square in the wall between the front office and the carpeted rear area. Gooper arranged file cabinets. A sign painter applied letters to the modern glass door.

Quack came in and rubbernecked. He whistled appreciatively. "The place looks official, now! Very nice! But, Ace, I saw something odd in the theater district."

"Do tell," Ace said mildly, jotting numbers on a pad of paper.

"I saw a poster for a symphony concert. The featured work is a piano concerto."

"Ah." Ace pursed her lips.

"Ace? Are you playing cagey with me? The pianist was listed as Cecilia Carroway!"

"Yes. Well." Ace rubbed at the back of her neck.

"Ace? Spill it!"

Ace exhaled long, inflating her cheeks with the air of resignation. "That was all arranged before I crashed. Symphonies have long lead times."

The slender blond actor waved his arms, spluttering helplessly. "But, but, you play piano? You play piano *concertos*?"

Gooper chuckled from across the room. "Now, some of us, we already knew of Ace's musical prowess on account of — *we pay attention!*"

"But I thought you were a medical doctor!" Quack accused Ace.

"I specialize in soft tissue surgery, but I'm sure I could manage a bit of orthopedic surgery, too, in a pinch."

"Ace, you astound me. You really do." Quack shook his head from side to side in wonder. Because he was *Hamlet* each night, his blond beard was trimmed to Van Dyke style mustache and goatee, with cheeks shaved bare.

Gooper squinted at the main office door, where the painter was lettering. He said, "Ace? Weren't we going ter be Acme Detective Agency or somesuch? 'E's writin' *your* name on the door."

"I scrapped the idea of going incognito. I didn't cancel the concert, for one. For another, all sorts of people already know. People at Carroway Shipping, estate lawyers, people I bump into on the street. I can't stop the inevitable. The door will say 'C. Carroway and Associates.' I think we're ready for trouble. We're certainly ready to take cases. What do you say, Gooper? Are you ready for trouble?"

Gooper waggled his bushy red eyebrows. "Cor! That's an understatement, that is!"

Quack pouted. "I have a feeling me playing *Hamlet* is going to mean I will miss some fun."

Bert arrived, accompanied by a man in a trench coat and hat. As usual, Bert wore a snappy suit and hat as if he was on his way to model at a photography studio. The man in the trench coat, on the other hand, seemed permanently rumpled. He slouched in, not removing his hat.

"This is ONI agent Franklin Case," Bert said, frowning sidelong at the craggy-faced, unshaven man in the trench coat. "I haven't seen his badge."

"I'm legit, chum. Call me Ironclad." Agent Case approached Ace and thrust an Office of Naval Intelligence badge in her direction. "We meet again, Miss Carroway. I need a few words. In private. Won't take long."

The sign painter snapped his toolbox shut and announced, "All done, ma'am. Have a nice day."

Ace waved to the painter. "Thanks, Charlie. Take care, now." The painter left. Ace regarded Ironclad for a few moments, then said, "Everyone here works for Carroway and Associates. You still need to talk in private?"

The agent shrugged. "Guess not."

Ace nodded. "Rank of Commander, it says here."

"Yeah, sort of. Not that they'd ever be dumb enough to let me command a ship, but I've been reassigned civilian. So it's Agent Case. Ironclad will do, though. We might be working together."

"Oh? Why do you say that?"

"I'd like to request you and your boys," Ironclad's eyes flicked from Bert to Gooper to Quack, "keep your eyes peeled. Share what you find out, and we're working together, kinda by definition."

Ace asked, "Eyes peeled for what?"

Agent Case slouched with apparent unconcern. "Smuggler's Crossroads, it's called. We don't know a whole lot more, except it's somewhere in this neighborhood. It's some kind of meetin' place for international criminals. A deal-makin' spot. Maybe smuggling, like the name suggests. We won't know until we find it and sting it."

Ace said, "We're new in town. What makes you think we'll make any progress?"

"Hey, now! We're observant." Bert said.

Ironclad produced a toothpick from the recesses of his trench coat pocket and inserted it into the corner of his mouth. "Seein' as how you're opening a detective agency in the neighborhood, I might've come to say hello anyway, but I happen to know somethin' extra. Now that you're alive again, Miss Carroway, you are a witness in a particular open case I'm following. The Darko Dor investigation."

Gooper, Quack, and Bert all closed ranks around Ace in a united front. Gooper flexed his massive shoulders as if preparing for a fight then and there. "Darko Dor? Got our attention right an' proper, that did!"

"What do you know about Darko Dor?" Quack wondered.

Agent Case squinted at Quack. "You look like Hamlet or something. As for Darko Dor, he paid a visit to Smuggler's Crossroads. He hired some henchmen out of there a few months back, tryin' to kill Miss Carroway, here."

"I can vouch for that," Ace said.

The rumpled agent nodded. "Those birds sang, but they said they were blindfolded whenever they arrived or left Smuggler's Crossroads." He offered Ace a business card. "If you find out anything, call me. At this point, we'll even chase rumors."

The associates exchanged glances, then nodded all around. Ace said, "Eyes peeled, it is, Agent Case. What about Mrs. Gemrock? Was she mugged?"

Ironclad nodded and flipped his toothpick from one side of his mouth to the other. "Probably a Ratface job. He pinched her jewelry and her cash, but he left alone the bulky items like her mink and purse."

"Ratface?" Bert said.

Ironclad thrust his hands deeper in his coat pockets and slouched. "Yeah. I don't know a lot. ONI's jurisdiction is international crime. We don't track muggers or robbers, so you gotta ask the police. This guy wears a mask that looks like a rat head. I hear the police are tearin' their hair out, but he don't leave 'em any clues."

After goodbyes, the trench-coated agent left.

"Ha-ha! I almost burst out laughing when he called you Hamlet!" Bert grinned at Quack.

Quack didn't rise to Bert's baiting. His eyebrows knit in puzzlement and he asked Ace, "Did I hear right? Is his name really Ironclad Case?"

CHAPTER II

At the hospital, the receptionist glanced at Ace's face. "Are you checking yourself in?"

Ace inwardly counted to ten. "No. I am here to see if I can visit Sarah Gemrock."

"Oh! I see." The receptionist buried her heated cheeks in the logbook and then timidly reported, "She's gone home."

"Address, please."

Half an hour later, Ace tapped the filigreed door knocker of an uptown apartment. A trim gentleman answered. The indentations of spectacles flanked his nose, though no lenses perched there to magnify his astute eyes. Dark hair sprinkled with gray partially covered a malformed ear. Like most people meeting Ace since her crash, his eyes flicked to her scars. After a split second of concern, or even horror, his face relaxed, and he gave a relieved smile, as if what he saw in Ace's scars was better than what he had imagined. "Yes?"

"Cecilia Carroway. Is this the Gemrock residence?"

"Oh! Miss Carroway! Come in! What a lovely surprise. I'm Cheswick Thornby, a … erm … a friend of Sarah's. Come in! Sarah's just on the couch."

A sunny voice sang from inside, "Is that Ace? Bring her in, Cheswick!"

Sarah Gemrock reclined on a divan in the sitting room amid a gentle perfume of freshly cut flowers. She had fixed her hair to cover the goose egg swelling on her head. She held her undamaged hand out toward Ace. Ace took it warmly in both of hers.

"Cheswick's been pampering me," Sarah said.

Thornby said mildly, "Doctor's orders."

"You'd pamper me anyway."

"True enough."

Sarah turned to Ace. "I'm feeling ever so much better. I don't know why I have to stay still and quiet."

"Doctor's orders," Thornby said again, a twinkle in his eye.

Ace said, "Your doctor is perfectly right. Concussions easily get worse instead of better. I'm glad to see you have help, Mrs. Gemrock."

"Oh, Cheswick's a dear. I'm lucky to have him." Sarah hastened to add, "I mean, he's a very dear friend, not a husband! Garrett's been dead these five years and I'm a widow. Oh! Me and my mouth!" The middle aged woman commenced blushing like a teen.

Thornby blushed, too. He gazed gently at Sarah. "The way my heart was in my throat when I found out you were robbed and beaten, Sarah, I learned how much you mean to me, and it's a lot."

"Oh!" Sarah said, a delighted smile spreading across her face.

Thornby said, "Greater than Avagadro's number."

"He's a chemist," Sarah explained, "They talk like that. I think it's charming."

"Very romantic," Ace agreed.

The days before the symphony concert passed swiftly. Since the official name of the detective agency was "C. Carroway and Associates," the five men realized that they, collectively, were "the associates." Tombstone installed radio gear in a fast new four-door roadster. He taught the associates the ins and outs of radio transmission in the fourth floor communications room, now festooned with an array of electrical devices.

"This is all so modern, I feel like I'm in the future. My head spins," Quack remarked as he toyed with a phosphor-coated cathode ray tube.

Ace said, "It's the one advantage we can count on, Quack. We want to stay a step ahead on the technical side."

Quack tapped his own temple. "My headache now will pay off later?"

"That's the idea."

The remainder of the fourth floor became operational as well. Ace stocked the laboratory with an eye toward metallurgy, chemistry, physics and microbiology. The sterile "infirmary" was really an operating theater to rival that of any hospital, so ultramodern were its tools. First thing, Ace imported a grand piano and placed it in the library. Thereafter, she spent hours each day practicing. The library shelves filled with reference books.

Sam dug up the newspaper trail on Ratface. He reported to Ace between practice sessions. "He first appeared six months ago, memsahib. He has robbed four individuals and two small stores to date, if you count

Mrs. Gemrock. His mask is not very realistic when seen in good light, but apparently very lifelike at night."

Ace asked, "Does he use a club?"

"A small club or blackjack, yes. So far, he has used it at least once at each robbery."

"What is Mrs. Gemrock's background?"

"Her name was Mangrove before she married mining baron Garrett Gemrock in 1905. He was killed in a Pennsylvania tunnel collapse in 1916, and she has lived in New York since. The couple had no children."

"Thank you, Sam."

"It is my pleasure, memsahib."

"You're never going to call me just plain Ace, are you?"

"Not without suitable ornamentation, Lady Ace." Sam dimpled serenely.

Ace gave up. Upon passing Mrs. Figgins, Ace paused and looked at her with suspicion. "Mrs. Figgins, you look like the cat that ate the cream. Did something just happen?"

"Nothing much, Miss Carroway. I sent a fellow away, that's all."

"Who?"

"Some young man. He didn't have a case, he just wanted to see you."

"Ah. Erm. Tall? Dark? Gray eyes? Good-looking?"

"Yes, that's about right." Mrs. Figgins bent and rummaged in her waste bin. She retrieved a calling card, and read it out loud. "Jeremy Braggs." Mrs. Figgins's face scrunched as if she had just bitten into a lemon. "Did you want to see him, after all? The card just has a name, no address."

Ace stroked a hand along the scarred portion of her face. In faraway tones, she said, "No, you did exactly as required, Mrs. Figgins. Good work."

The only "case" the new, unlisted detective agency handled was a distraught eight-year-old. The boy kept his head and knew how to read. He followed the detective agency signs in the 301 Wall building until he discovered Gooper, who happened to be in the lobby. The boy, tearful and snuffling, told Gooper that he had lost his parents. Gooper plopped a bowler hat on his head, took the boy by the hand, and led him outside. As they stood on the busy street corner and scanned the crowd, the massive, mustachioed Gooper launched into a story, keeping his words short. The yarn concerned a travelling rugby team that accidentally found themselves faced off against an American baseball team.

"Did they play?" asked the child, round-eyed.

"Oh, aye!"

"Who won?"

"'Oo were the victors? Well, now. It would've been a sure bet on the rugby team, except for one thing."

"What?"

"The Americans all had bats. Injected new life into the ruck, those bats did."

Before the boy got too suspicious, Gooper spotted

the frantic parents and flagged them down.

On the day of the concert, Quack was in dress rehearsal for Hamlet and could not attend. Bert, Sam, Gooper, and Tombstone dressed in tuxedos. Tombstone called his a "monkey suit" and griped about how the bow tie was throttling him to death.

"Oi hope it don't," Gooper told him deadpan. "Throttlin' you 's my prerogative!"

At the concert hall, Bert surprised them by showing up with an attractive redhead on his arm. "Gentlemen. This is my good friend Suzanne Hawksworth, down from Boston for the concert. Suzanne, these are Sam, Tombstone, and Gooper. Trust me on that. They get confused if you call them by their actual names."

"A pleasure, gentlemen," Suzanne said, laughter in her voice.

The group sat on plush seats in the middle of the ornate symphony hall. Gooper and Tombstone confessed discomfort at the formal setting and ignorance about concert etiquette. Bert and Sam showered them with advice both helpful and unhelpful.

They hushed up as the concert began. A prelude by Liszt and a symphony by Sibelius were first on the program. Bert and Sam, by virtue of quick reflexes, managed to keep Gooper and Tombstone from clapping between movements. At intermission, Tombstone groaned, "Aww, shucks! I wanna hear Ace play, but they turned the lights back on!"

A nearby gentleman in a cravat said, "I want to hear her, too! I have heard good things about this pianist. A golden touch on the keyboard, they say, but she seldom gives concerts. A woman of mystery!"

Bert chuckled. "Yes, that's a good description."

"An' that ain't the half of it!" Tombstone said.

"I'm here to see if she's real," Suzanne said.

Stagehands dressed in black gingerly wheeled a concert grand piano to the front of the stage. They fussed with it interminably. At long last, the lights dimmed again, and the orchestra tuned. The conductor and a tall woman in a flowing red sleeveless dress emerged from stage right, to enthusiastic applause. It wasn't until she sat down at the piano bench that it dawned on Tombstone. "Good golly! That's Ace!"

"Shhh!" scolded the gentleman in the cravat.

"Oh, my! She's real, down to the scars," Suzanne whispered to Bert.

The orchestra began to play. The theme of Chopin's second piano concerto washed over the audience. Then the pianist joined in, interjecting spritely flourishes. Her fingers fluttered, and her arms moved in mesmerizing, flowing wavelike motions. The music rose and fell hypnotically, holding the audience spellbound. The final movement was dancelike and uplifting. When the final cadence rang to silence, the entire room seemed to hold its breath. Then the audience rose to its feet, roaring and clapping maniacally. The four associates and Suzanne stood, too, and clapped, expressions of wonder on their faces.

And then the chaos commenced.

CHAPTER 12

The conductor raised the orchestra to their feet. He then insisted that Ace take a solo bow while he himself applauded. As she straightened up, a dapper, tuxedoed man offered her a bouquet of flowers from the front edge of the stage. She bent and gathered the bouquet into the crook of her elbow.

From somewhere overhead, a baritone voice hailed theatrically, "No! My lady! Do not take the flowers!"

A caped figure posed at the top corner of the stage-leg, where only riggers should go. Once all eyes were upon him, he leapt into space and plummeted toward the ground. The crowd gasped, but he also clutched a rope. As he gracefully rode the rope through the air, his cape undulated behind.

He arced over the center of the stage, dropped lightly to the floor, and drew himself into a tall pose, chest out. He was masked in black, and his long mouse brown hair was pulled back in a ponytail. Red satin lined his cape. A red satin cummerbund wrapped around his trim waist.

He bowed with a courtly swish of his cape and boldly addressed the startled Ace.

"Never fear, milady! I am here to rescue you!" To the audience, he cried, "And I am here to save you all! From the fire!"

There was a pause. The audience tittered in uncertainty. The conductor seemed at a loss and the orchestra musicians seemed entertained. The man who had given Ace the flowers hopped up on stage and headed for the caped man, his pose aggressive.

The masked man cried again, "I said, 'the fire!' The fire, confound it!" At the approach of the man in the tuxedo, he protested in noble, aggrieved tones, "Oh, no you don't! I'm rescuing the damsel, not you!"

The masked man gave the approaching man a shove. The man in the tuxedo tumbled to the stage floor, then rolled off the stage altogether. The audience babbled in consternation.

At that moment, from the rear of the stage there was a muted concussion followed by hissing noises. The trombone section all but disappeared within a billow of smoke. Various musicians protested.

"Hey!"

"What's the big idea?"

"Ack!"

"Kof!"

The masked man crowed, "Ah, ha! You see? Fire. Better late than never. Fire, I say! Come, my dear. Will you come with me to safety?" He circled the grand piano toward Ace.

Bert, Suzanne, Tombstone, Sam, and Gooper began moving, as did the rest of the audience, some of whom took up the cry, "Fire!" The trombones, tubas, and baritones cursed between coughs. A few people stayed seated and said, "It's a smoke bomb! Some joker thinks it's funny." Most preferred to escape the theater in a hubbub of angry mutterings.

Ace upticked an eyebrow at the masked gallant as he tried to put an arm around her waist. He abruptly changed tactics and bowed low instead. "Do forgive my headstrong impertinence, noble lady. I assure you it is only your safety I think of. Come away, please! The fire! The poisoned flowers!"

The man in the tuxedo leapt back to the stage and pounded toward the caped swashbuckler. "Get away from Cecilia Carroway, you madman!" The orchestra conductor also closed in on the masked man, his face livid.

Cornered, the caped fellow abruptly turned with a billow of scarlet and ran backstage. He wove a path through bewildered first violins on his way. "Forget me not, dear Lady! For I am and will always be true to you!"

The gentleman from the audience pounded after him. The conductor followed, too, for a few moments, shaking his fist-enclosed baton.

After a moment of reflection, Ace flopped the flowers on the piano bench and joined the pursuit in a billow of silky scarlet fabric.

The four associates danced down the middle of the hall, over the seats, feet spearing down on vacated seat cushions. The aisles were full of people, and Suzanne was left behind in the pandemonium. The four associates rolled up on stage. They, too, dodged bewildered musicians on their way to the back entrance of the concert hall.

Guided by a steady stream of shouting from the man that had given Ace flowers, they burst out into the chilly alley behind the concert hall.

Across the alley loomed a five-story tenement. A metal fire escape zigzagged up its stone walls. The masked man clattered upon it, climbing, already three stories up. The dapper man pursued a couple of stories below. The conductor had given up the chase. Ace minced along in third place using an awkward tiptoe gait. Evidently, her shoes were giving her trouble.

The chase was on! The masked man found enough breath to brassily proclaim, "You'll never catch Darryl Dashing, demon of derring do!" and, "Despair not, milady! If he gets his claws into you, call my name and I will rescue you!"

Ace paused on a landing. She looked up, raised a finger, and opened her mouth.

"Fleet of foot! Quick of hand!" crowed Darryl Dashing.

Ace wagged her head in perplexity and resumed climbing.

Ace's four associates piled on the fire escape and swarmed up, cutting into the masked man's lead. The masked man gained the roof and skipped his way across.

The dapper gentleman, Ace, and the four associates arrived at almost the same moment, spilling out on the roof, huffing and blowing.

There was an odd tableau for a moment. The masked man stood facing them on the opposite side of the roof, one hand on his heart, the other holding his cape-edge. He smirked at the ragged line of well-dressed pursuers. "I'm flattered at the attention, my friends, and I admit that it has been an invigorating dollop of exercise, but now it is time to end it. *Au revoir!*"

He unhooked his cape and whipped it off in such theatrical style that Quack, had he been present, might have taken notes.

The tuxedoed man strode forward and command-ed, "Now, stop right there! I want a word. You've probably broken a law or two, but that's— whoa! Stop!"

The masked man stepped to the brickwork at building edge and jumped!

Rumbles and rattles arose from below, but no screams and no sounds of wet thuds from street level.

Everyone rushed over and peered over the side.

"It's a garbage slide!" blurted Tombstone.

Sure enough, it appeared that the masked man had slid down a tube like those used at construction sites to toss rubble down.

There was a metallic bang. The slide vibrated and slumped slightly.

The dapper man splayed his hands out in warning, "Do not jump! He has separated the slide in the middle."

Everyone squinted down and over. New York was never completely dark but the gloom hung heavy down in the alley. Only after long moments did their eyes grudgingly adjust. There was the faintest of clack-clack sounds and a tiny figure ran to the corner of the next building over, at ground level. The escaping man paused to sweep a bow, then whisked away. The garbage chute had indeed separated. The bottom half sagged to one side. The top half emptied in mid-air, two stories above the unyielding pavement.

Ace said, "Yes. No one follow. He has escaped."

"Durn rascally coyote!" Tombstone griped.

Bert picked the cast-off cape up from the rooftop.

"Call me opinionated, but I think New Yorkers are off their rorkers."

Sam corrected, "The phrase is 'off their rockers,' I think, Bert."

"I like it better my way," said Bert darkly.

The tuxedoed gentleman said, "Miss Carroway, are you alright? What a strange episode!" He bowed.

"Mr. Braggs. We meet again." The four associates' eyes bugged out as Braggs captured one of Ace's hands and kissed her knuckles. They were even more flabbergasted a moment later when Ace curtsied, her scarlet dress undulating gently.

Gooper grumbled under his breath, "Crikey. Robust constitution Oi may 'ave, but Oi'm numb from all th' shocks, regardless!"

"Thank you for the flowers. They were lovely." Ace said.

"Not as lovely as your brilliant interpretation of Chopin, Miss Carroway. I was simply bowled over. As for the flowers, I shall try again to deliver them. At some quieter moment. But for now, I wonder if we should descend? It's quite chilly up here," Jeremy Braggs gestured toward the fire escape.

The four associates glared at him in the semidarkness. He was a handsome fellow, trim and confident, resplendent in his tuxedo.

"Yeah. Let's git." Tombstone said through clenched teeth.

The four continued to chafe as Braggs insisted on escorting Ace down the fire escape. Ace threaded a hand through the crook of his elbow. They followed along until Ace ducked into her dressing room at the back of the hall. They spread out like bodyguards, standing in a line in front of the door. They crossed their arms, jutted their lower jaws out, and widened their stances.

Braggs took the hint. "Right. Well. Nice to meet you chaps, but I'd best be off. Do take care."

Suzanne found the party as Jeremy Braggs departed. Her eyes widened after she scanned the passing Braggs. She inspected the row of bodyguards and shook her head from side to side. "Never a dull moment with you lot, is there? I couldn't keep up."

Bert said, "Sorry, Suzanne."

Suzanne took a second look. The whole row of men all but crackled with electricity. They seemed vivid and flushed with energy after the chase. Suzanne's intuition clicked: These were born adventurers. Restless while resting, only in motion were they paradoxically at peace.

"Who *was* that man?" Suzanne asked, looking back after Braggs.

"His name's mud," grumbled Bert.

"Well, he's very handsome. Set my heart aflutter."

Bert spluttered inarticulately.

Suzanne slipped a hand in the crook of Bert's elbow. "Oh, Bert. Jealous?" She batted her eyelashes at him.

"'Is name's Jeremy Braggs, Miss Hawkworth," Gooper said, "But Oi'd like ter know about the acrobat an' the smoke bomb."

Sam said, "What *was* that about? No one does things for no reason, but this masked man's motivations are not obvious to my mind."

"Attention-grabber's my bet," Tombstone drawled.

"'E bore a striking resemblance to the Scarlet Pimpernel!" Gooper chortled.

Bert said, "But is he dangerous? He did break the law. Inciting a panic is illegal. Even in lawless New York."

The door opened.

"The pianist is gone and Lady Ace reappears!" Sam announced. Ace stood framed by the rectangle of the doorway. She wore a loose fitting flight suit with a wide belt and carried a scarlet dress over her arm. Heeled shoes dangled from her hand.

"We meet properly at last," Suzanne said, extending a hand.

"Ace, meet Suzanne Hawksworth," Bert said.

Ace shook her hand. "Suzanne. A pleasure. I hope you will accept my apology for what happened in Boston. I never intended to frighten."

Suzanne put on a wry expression. "What it is, is that some girls frighten too easily. No apology necessary."

Ace and Suzanne grinned at each other for a moment. Ace scanned the row of stalwart associates. "I don't believe I will give a concert again for a while."

Sam said, "You are not developing an allergy to mayhem, are you, Lady Ace?"

"No, not that. More foundational. It's the shoes. I wonder if my toes will ever be the same."

Chapter 13

The next day at the lab, Quack learned of the scandalous goings-on. He was glum about missing the chase.

"I caught a rumor about Smuggler's Crossroads, though," he said.

"Eureka! I knew all actors were shady!" Bert snapped his fingers triumphantly.

Quack shot Bert a withering glare. "Stuff it, Brat. Backstage, there's a stage hand with a reputation. Ex-convict, they say. He's keeping clean as far as we can tell, but he's not very social. I went and asked him. He winced and said, 'Can't talk about Smuggler's Crossroads.' And that's all I could get."

"It's something. If nothing else, it tells us the place is real," Ace said.

Quack said, "Yeah, it must be real. Say, about last night, did anyone check the flowers to see if they were booby-trapped or something?"

Ace answered, "Perfectly ordinary flowers. There was a timed smoke bomb behind the trombone section; a cheap alarm clock tied to a bundle of over-the-counter fireworks."

Bert handed a pocket watch to Gooper. "I found this in the inside pocket of his cape. What did he say his name was? Oh, yes, Darryl Dashing. Well, anyway, I found this watch on a chain, and it's a nice watch. I bet he's missing it, by now. It's got a symbol on the back. Gooper, it's about your style; it's biological."

Gooper turned the watch over with thick fingers and squinted at it, mustache bristling. "I behold an artistic representation of a woody perennial. Not just any tree, neither. Look at tha' trunk! It's an African Baobab, wot they call the Tree o' Life."

"Any idea why it might be on the back of somebody's pocket watch?"

"Not a clue, guv'nor! I'd better go research it."

Sam said, "I will inquire at the concert hall. Perhaps someone knows him there."

"I'll check for news of masked madmen at the newspaper office," said Quack.

Bert said, "I'll take this cape around to local tailors and see if they recognize it. Maybe they can tell me who bought it."

"Excellent," said Ace. "Thank you for pitching in, gentlemen. I have no additional clues for you to follow up. I know nothing beyond the obvious: He is farsighted but left his glasses off, is left handed, works a desk job, and owns a puppy." Ace frowned at the far wall, deep in thought.

The associates stood with slack jaws and uncomprehending expressions. They rubbed at their chins and furrowed their foreheads. Finally, Gooper hesitantly said, "'Ow ... 'ow d'ye know 'e owns a puppy?"

Ace blinked back to the present. "His shoes. Chewed-on, with tooth marks visible. His eyes didn't focus well when he was close to me, hence farsightedness. His left hand was ink-stained from writing. When you are a lefty, you drag your hand across what you have just written, you see."

Tomstone's head, shoulders, and Stetson poked

through the doorway. "Ah got th' capacitors, Ace."

Ace nodded at the cowboy electrician. "Tombstone and I are off to the hangar to install more radio equipment. Good luck bagging the dashing Darryl Dashing. Let's meet back here this afternoon and compare notes."

♠ ♠ ♠

They gathered in the third floor lounge to share their findings. Mrs. Figgins took advantage of their presence in her bailiwick. Knowing they would handle any clients that came in, she turned her back on the door to heat water for tea.

No one had bagged Darryl Dashing. But Quack grinned and waved scraps of newsprint at Ace and the associates. "I found a pair of newspaper articles that might describe him. Six months ago, a masked man climbed a tree and rescued a cat."

Bert wrinkled his nose. "Doesn't have to be him. Lots of loose screws rattling around New York."

Quack smugly retorted, "Wait. There is also this. A masked man chased a purse snatcher a year ago in Queens. He recovered the purse, then posed for a picture with the grateful owner. The picture was printed and here it is. What do you think?"

"That's 'im!" Gooper exclaimed.

"Yep. Same mask, same nose, same chin dimple," Tombstone contributed.

"Isn't he a handsome devil?" Ace said mildly.

"Lady Ace, are you feeling alright?" Sam wondered.

"Perfectly fine, thank you. Bert, did you trace the cloak?"

Bert nodded. "Success, and yet no success. The theatrical tailor down the street remembered a man. He didn't wear a mask, but he gave his name as Darryl Dashing and paid in cash."

Sam said, "The slide was built so that the first person coming down tripped a lever which made the slide separate into two. The bottom half flopped over, and the top half emptied out in midair, two stories up. I asked the building superintendent, but he did not remember when the tube was installed, or who installed it.

"I interviewed staff members at the concert hall, to no avail. The property master said he was surprised by the masked man. He had not seen him before. No one observed anyone suspicious or saw the smoke bomb beforehand."

Gooper was last to report. "Oi got nowhere. The baobab tree ... well, I think I've seen the symbol before. Bugger me, I can't think o' where, though. The jeweler said the watch can't be more than five years old. He said a lot o' jewelers could've done the engraving, an' that it was nice, quality work."

Ace reached for the watch. "It strikes me as commemorative. Like a watch given at retirement, perhaps. The symbol would relate to the organization. Does that jog anything loose?"

Gooper's large, wild, red mustache twitched for a while, then he shook his head. "Nar. Nought shook loose."

"Excuse me," said a voice.

The five swiveled their heads as one. A tall man stood by the door, dapper and clean. He carried a bouquet of flowers. His hat tilted jauntily and a perfect white triangle of a handkerchief accented the front pocket of his new suit.

"Jeremy Braggs, what a pleasant surprise," Ace said.

Mrs. Figgins turned in place by her desk to sourly regard Braggs as she dipped a tea bag in a china cup.

Braggs seemed impervious to the disfavor of Mrs. Figgins. "Good afternoon, Miss Carroway. Good afternoon, gentlemen."

He thrust the bouquet of flowers forward. "For you, Miss Carroway. Truly, the performance still plays on in my head. I don't know if I will ever forget it."

The associates rumbled assorted bullfroggish attempts at pleasantries. Ace glided over and accepted the flowers. "They are lovely. Thank you very much."

Braggs bowed. "You are most welcome, Miss Carroway. Miss Carroway, erm, I should very much like to chat in private some time. Do you ever eat lunch out?"

"I don't, normally," Ace replied. The bullfrog chorus fidgeted.

"Ah, I see. Well, will you make an exception in my case?"

Ace glanced at Mrs. Figgins, then back to Braggs. "Some other time, perhaps."

"Well, I'm disappointed, but that's that. Ta-ta!" Braggs bowed, smiled whitely, turned on his heel, and exited.

The bullfrogs all visibly deflated after the door shut. Ace bent her head to sample the fragrance of the flowers.

After inhaling their subtle perfume, she found a whole row of eyes on her. A line creased between her brows. "Don't you lot have something else to do?"

A moment later, they all did. Shouts erupted from outside.

Braggs protested in tones of panic, "Go away! Stop waving that at me! I'm not - ow! Hey!"

There was an answering voice, bold and brassy.

"Do not dare to defy Darryl Dashing, you poor, puny peon!"

CHAPTER 14

Ace dodged a sudden stampede of associates in order to hand off the flowers to Mrs. Figgins, then followed. At the top of the stairs, masked Darryl Dashing threatened Jeremy Braggs with a fencing sabre.

"Goodly citizens, kindly do not interfere, for I am a man scorned, and I demand satisfaction!" cried the masked man, now cape-less. He kept moving, his sabre pointed at Braggs as he pranced in the mode of a fencer, with back foot squared off and front foot pointed forward.

"Will you just ... bug off? Madman!" said Braggs.

"Yew want we should rush 'im?" Gooper wondered as Ace joined the party.

"Oh, very well, knaves! Have it your way, but I shall never give up! Ha!"

On the "ha!" the masked swordsman thrust forward.

Braggs cried out and lurched back, clutching at his chest.

Darryl Dashing turned tail and ran rabbitlike down the stairwell. The office was two flights of stairs up from ground level.

All five associates abandoned the reeling Braggs and gave chase. Ace hesitated, eying him. He said, "I'm all right. See if you can get that menace locked up!"

Ace jogged off down the stairs.

This time the chase did not ascend to the rooftops. The black-and-red-clad swordsman dodged through pedestrian and automobile traffic with apparent glee. Ace's associates pursued pell mell, full of chaotic energy. Ace padded along at the rear.

A block and a half later, Dashing veered into an alley and put on speed. When the party of detectives arrived, he was disappearing down a manhole. He held the manhole cover tilted up and called, "Until we meet again, and that impertinent boor Braggs is duly fried in oil!" With his speech delivered, and his pursuit nearly on top of him, he popped underground. The manhole cover gave two grating clunk sounds.

Gooper reached down to rip the manhole cover off. He grunted, but nothing happened. "Cor blimey! Oi'm obfuscated!" he muttered, trying again, and again, bulging muscles straining.

"I believe Darryl Dashing locked it." Ace stood at ease.

"Wot?"

"I agree with Gooper," Sam said, "One does not lock a manhole cover. They are merely made of heavy iron so that they sit immovably."

"I think we will find that this one is equipped with a simple lock. Gooper, would you please locate other nearby manholes and see if you can backtrack to this one and unlock it? I'd like to see the mechanism."

Gooper jogged off. Sam frowned at the serene Ace for a while, then burst out, "Lady Ace? Are you not maddened? Is this not frustrating?"

Ace clasped her hands behind her back. "Yes and no. Perhaps you have heard of some recent developments in the physics of the very small. The atom, previously thought to be the smallest indivisible unit of matter, is now known to have subunits.

"Furthermore, experiments in this realm are very difficult, because the performance of the experiment often alters the result of it. One can see this in more ordinary situations, too. For example, if you try to catch a thistledown floating on the air, the very motion of your hand causes air currents that drive the thistledown away."

"Ah dun get it,' Tombstone said.

Ace laughed. "Well, let me finish my analogy. This Darryl Dashing is a puzzle, and we haven't figured out the solution. If we catch him now, we may, in fact, *never* figure out the solution. But if we let the plot develop, the clues will pile up, and the answer will emerge. Now are you with me?"

"Ohhhhhh!" Tombstone nodded.

"I disagree. He's a menace!" Bert growled.

"Not really, Bert," Ace said, "Did you get a good look at his sabre?"

"Sure. Quack and I fenced together in college, just with foils or epées, not the heavier sabres," Bert said.

"What did you notice?" Ace persisted.

"What do you mean? It had a hilt guard and a sharp pointy end. It wasn't antique or fancy or anything."

"Almost correct. In fact, it was a sport sabre, such as your college fencing club would have on hand. So the point was not sharp, at all. The tip was blunted. He did not, could not have hurt Jeremy Braggs."

Bert groaned, "Alright, he's not a menace. He's a showboat, though! And as irritating as Quack when he recites Shakespeare over and over."

"'Though this be madness, yet there is method in't,'" blithely quoted Quack.

"Oh, I'm gonna punch you in the *Hamlet* beard!" Bert curled his fingers into fists.

The manhole cover emitted twin clunk sounds, then popped up and slid over. Gooper's pale face framed with flaming red hair poked up out of the circular hole.

Tombstone said, "Ew! Somethin' ugly's comin' outta the sewer!"

Gooper grinned at Tombstone. "Oi found some lizard playmates for you, guv! Want ter take a look?"

"Ah'll pass," Tombstone said. Gooper waggled his shaggy red eyebrows in triumph.

Ace flipped the cover over to examine the underside. Two iron brackets had been welded on. Flat iron bars sat in the brackets, and could be slid back and forth. When the cover sat in its collar, the bars could slip into a pair of holes just underground that had been strategically dug out for the purpose.

"Not complex, but very effective," Ace summarized. "And also, preplanned."

"'E stymied us most efficaciously!" agreed Gooper. His bulging shoulders bumped the sides of the manhole, so he had to twist like a hunchback to climb to street level.

"Very fresh welds, too. Like they were done yesterday," Ace said. Her eyes defocused, staring past infinity. The air filled with a low contralto humming, seeming to come from all sides.

Gooper recognized it. It was the sound Ace made when she'd figured something out. "Wot? Wot is it?"

he eagerly asked.

But Ace shook her head in the negative. "I can't be sure, so I'll keep quiet for now."

Quack raised a hand to stroke his mustache. But the gesture also hid the movement of his lips as he whispered, "Act casual. Stay natural, but there's a guy spying on us."

CHAPTER 15

Bert was facing away from the street. "Behind me?"

Quack kept stroking his mustache. "Yes. Across the street, behind a parked car. Brown jacket. Tweed, maybe."

Ace kept fiddling with the welded brackets on the manhole cover. "Shall we escort him back to the office? Gooper and Tombstone, leave the alley and bear left. Argue as you go, I'm sure you can figure out how. Bert and Quack, the same, but you two bear right. Sam, you and I will stay here. In three minutes, we'll spring the trap. Clear?"

Tombstone said, "Clear as Texas skies!"

Gooper said, "Clear as me conscience after I mash the stick man to a pile of twigs."

Quack laughed. "Argue with Brat? How novel!"

Bert warmed up to the task immediately. "That's Bert, you blubbering incompetent! How you ever passed an audition I'll never know."

Sam spoke a worried aside to Ace. "This behavior. I'm not sure I would encourage it, memsahib."

"It won't get violent," Ace said. "Or so I hope."

Four of the associates ambled in bickering pairs toward the street. Ace fiddled with the manhole cover as if it were a great mystery.

"Circle me, Sam. I want to see if the fellow is still there."

Sam dutifully walked around Ace. As Sam passed the line of sight, Ace used the cover to catch glimpses. The man in a brown suit loitered against the building, pretending to read a newspaper, though his eyes were staring straight ahead, not down at the newsprint.

"Thank you, Sam," said Ace. "He appears to be tracking one of us, and I'm going to make a wild speculation and guess it's me."

Sam kept pacing. "I can think of no reason a man in brown should have interest in me, Lady Ace. This man, I see that his clothing hangs loosely on his frame. Perhaps he bought his suit secondhand."

Ace stuffed the pair of metal bars into one of her many flight suit pockets and rolled the manhole cover back into place. "If we stroll toward him, he'll have to bury his head in his newspaper. He won't see the others closing in."

"Good thinking, memsahib."

The man in brown raised his newspaper higher as Ace and Sam approached, hiding his face as Ace predicted. Their timing was good. Ace and Sam crossed the street amid light traffic. On the sidewalk, Quack approached from one direction, and Tombstone and Gooper closed in from the other. Bert had vanished.

The man in brown spotted Gooper and Tombstone first. After a look at their grim faces, he bolted in the opposite way, his hand diving behind his suit lapel to frantically grope. With an involuntary yelp, he careened straight into Quack, and they both went down in a flurry of flying limbs. A pistol came loose and skittered across the sidewalk into the gutter.

The man sprang up with Quack in hot pursuit. The

others closed in.

"Stop!" Gooper bellowed.

"Where's Bert?" Tombstone said.

In an impeccably-timed sideways leap, the man in brown latched on to a passing sedan. A white-knuckled hand clutched the door handle and his feet found purchase on the broad running board. A triumphant grin split his hard-bitten face as he zoomed away from the clump of pursuers.

They raced after the car on foot. Ace sprinted ahead of the pack, but even her speed lagged behind the car's.

The car's driver yelled, "Hey! What's the big idea! Get off!" The brakes lights lit. Tire rubber squealed. The man in brown abandoned the slowing car. He managed to keep his feet. His luck with vehicles held. An oncoming flatbed truck happened to be passing, loaded ten feet high with pallets of boards. The man in brown nipped behind the truck and clambered up its bumper.

The driver of the truck was unaware. Gears clashed as he accelerated. As the truck passed Ace, she, too, reversed course. When she arrived at the rear of the truck, she dodged a savage kick. She dropped back for a moment to mull the situation over. The man in brown had the high ground and a firm grip, but the truck was accelerating and Ace didn't have long to decide on a strategy.

Meanwhile, Sam, Quack, Tombstone and Gooper slowed as the truck approached. Tombstone caught Gooper's eye. "Toss me up."

"One caber toss, comin' up!" Gooper said, squatting low and lacing his hands together at knee level.

Tombstone lifted his booted foot into Gooper's hand-laced stirrup. "Alley oop!" Tombstone leaped, and Gooper boosted in unison. Tombstone's lanky limbs windmilled as he flew through the air.

The truck blew by the remaining associates with Ace flying behind. She plucked a metal bar from her pocket and hefted it in her hand. It was heavy enough, but she hesitated. If she missed by an inch, it would not stun the man in brown, it would blind him in one eye. The man in brown caught sight of the metal bar, too. Worry sprang into his eye.

Ace cocked her hand back and pumped as if to throw. The man in brown flinched and ducked. The truck picked up speed. It was now or never for launching the metal bar.

A shadow darkened the man in brown. A gangly-limbed missile dropped from the back of the load.

"Yee-haw!" Tombstone whooped. His booted feet landed squarely on the tweed-coated spy's shoulders. The spy squawked. They both fell off the truck with Tombstone on top. They bounced and rolled over and over on the pavement, ending in moaning heaps.

The truck rumbled away. Everybody gathered around. Gooper helped Tombstone up, and Quack and Sam clamped onto the arms of the dazed man in brown.

A battered van pulled up behind the group, but the driver did not honk. Instead, he leaned out his window and asked in a Boston accent, "Need a lift?"

Sam blurted, "It's Bert!"

Quack grinned. "Pretty good timing, Brat."

Tombstone rubbed at bruised elbows and eyed

Bert, the driver of the van. "Tarnation! He went an' fetched the radio van."

Ace said, "Well, let's pile in, before we cause a traffic jam."

A few seconds later, it was done. With Bert behind the wheel, the rest surrounded the tweed-coated man on the floor of the van. Spools of wire and racks of tools competed for space with them.

Quack searched and removed a four-inch knife from a pocket crudely sewn into the man's vest. The man in brown sweated and trembled.

"Just drive around for now, Bert," Ace said.

"'Ow many knots can I tie in 'im?" Gooper said, smacking a meaty fist into an open palm over and over.

The man whined, "Lemme go. I ain't done nothin'!"

Ace said, "Sam? Did you have time to scan the wanted posters at the police station?"

Sam said, "Yes, memsahib."

"Go ahead, Sam. Can you identify him?"

"Yes, memsahib. He is probably Cockroach Carl."

The man's trembling grew so pronounced his teeth rattled.

"'Oo, now?" Gooper said.

"I agree, Sam. This is Cockroach, wanted for burglary and as accomplice to kidnapping."

"Who are you people? Don't turn me in! I'll do anything!"

Quack rifled through the man's thin wallet. "You have three dollars, Mr. Cockroach. I think any offer to pay us off lacks credibility."

"Please!"

Ace curled a fist in his shirt and inclined her scars toward him. She spoke in icy tones. "Tell us about Smuggler's Crossroads."

"Aiee!" Cockroach gasped. "I ain't allowed there! I never been there! I know a guy, though. Gristle. You could talk to Gristle. Or Ratface. You could talk to Ratface!"

Ace tightened her grip. "I said, tell us about Smuggler's Crossroads. What's new, there?"

"I'll talk! I'm talking! Lemme think! I heard Futa killed a guy."

"What guy and who's Futa?"

"Futa's the doorkeeper. I dunno where the door is, I swear! I dunno where, and I never saw Futa, whoever he is. Word is, he's huge. Like a Jap sumo wrestler, but meaner.

"They say he can break you in half. And he killed a guy for not knowing the password. I think the guy's name was Hooky or something. What does it matter? He's dead."

"Keep spilling, Cockroach."

"W-w-well, there's you. Ace Carroway."

"Go on."

Cockroach's trembling became almost palsy. "Black market bounties. Two of 'em came up a few days back. I heard Ratface and Gristle talkin' 'em over."

Ace stated, with no hint of a question, "You were casing my movements so you could kidnap me later."

Cockroach seemed incapable of coherent speech, but he nodded his head feverishly.

Gooper said, "Yer moniker is an insult to Blattodeans[2] all over the world."

Tombstone nodded. "An' cockroaches, too."

Ace didn't let up.

"Who's paying the bounty?"

"S-s-some foreigner. Lotta dees in his name. Dongo Doo or something."

Ace said, grimly, "Close enough. And who earned the second bounty?"

"A scientist. Um. Um. Thornby. Yeah, that's it. Thornby. Damn my eyes. In hindsight I shouldda staked out his place, not yours."

Ace's brows knitted. "Cheswick Thornby?"

"Yeah, that's him."

"Why Cheswick Thornby?"

"I dunno, lady. I dunno."

"Bert. Head to the police station. We've got a drop off."

At the police station, Ace pulled Sam aside. "Filing police reports will eat at least an hour, but time may be of the essence. Take a cab to Sarah Gemrock's apartment. Try to find Cheswick Thornby. Warn him."

"Assuredly, memsahib."

---

[2] Cockroaches fall under phylum Arthropoda, class Insecta, order Blattodea.

Chapter 16

ONI agent Franklin "Ironclad" Case waited back at the Wall Street & Broadway office. His rumpled trench coat leaned on the counter, facing Mrs. Figgins. Figgins gazed back over her half-moon glasses. An odd peace filled the room.

Ace and associates filed in, tall and short, wide and skinny, neat and sloppy.

Ironclad scanned the incoming parade and shook his head. "Hello, again. No offense, but if the lot of you were a box of chocolates, I'd be nervous about what flavors I'd get."

Bert looked left and right at his fellow associates. "Honestly, so would I."

Ace inquired, "To what do we owe the pleasure of this visit, Agent Case?"

The rumpled agent rubbed his unshaven jaw. "We questioned a pigeon the other day. The police caught him near here, so as a matter of routine we asked about Smuggler's Crossroads. After a day or so, the pidge sang like a sparrow. Or whatever bird it is that sings."

Gooper winced. "Ornithologist yew are not, guv."

"Go on," Quack said, fingering his Hamlet beard.

Ironclad said, "He didn't know about Smuggler's Crossroads in particular, but he'd heard some things.

He heard there was a black market price on a couple of people's heads."

"Oh, really?" Ace said, mildly.

Ironclad said, "Ace Carroway, for one."

Ace showed no reaction. "And the second one?"

Ironclad eyed Ace with suspicion. "Uh, a Great War defector. Ch—"

Bert cut him off, "Cheswick Thornby."

Ironclad squinted at Bert, in turn. "Well, yeah. And, rumor is, the guy footing the bill is—"

Tombstone finished for him. "Darko Dor."

Ironclad's face twisted in a vexed expression. "And here I thought I was delivering a stunner! How'd you know?"

Ace said, "Same way you found out. We interviewed a low-level crook. He's under glass, now. But what do you know about Cheswick Thornby? A defector, you said?"

The ONI agent stuffed his hands in his trench coat pockets and slouched. "That's what the bright boys told me on my way out of the office. Before open war broke out, Thornby invented a way to purify chlorine gas. When the Ottomans wanted to make a weapon out of it, he fled."

Ace asked, "Did he work with acids, by any chance? I noticed his ear was misshapen. I guessed acid burns, but not recent ones."

Ironclad said, "Acid gas, maybe. I dunno."

Ace said, "And Darko Dor wants him alive. Now, I'm worried."

"What's Dor up to, Ace?" Quack asked.

Ace gazed in thoughtful abstraction at Quack, worry wrinkling her brow. She pivoted toward reception.

"Mrs. Figgins, ring up Sarah Gemrock, please. Find out how to reach Cheswick Thornby."

"Yes, ma'am. And, ma'am?" Mrs. Figgins's finger was already spinning the rotary dial on the main line telephone.

Ace said, "Yes?"

"Don't get kidnapped, please. I like working here." Mrs. Figgins's mouth deviated from a straight line, microscopically. One could almost believe she was attempting to smile.

A hoarse voice rasped from the office door. "Sahibs!"

Sam clung to the doorway to keep himself upright. His suit was scuffed, dirt-smeared, and tattered. Blood streamed from his temple down his brown cheek and neck to stain his collar and suit.

Tombstone and Gooper ran to support him.

"Sam! You all right, there, pardner?"

"Wot 'appened?"

Sam's pain-blurred eyes found Ace. "Lady Ace! Mr. Thornby has been abducted!"

CHAPTER 17

In the infirmary, Sam sat surrounded by the associates. Ironclad Case kept his hands in his pockets and examined the sterilizers, lights, and pumps with a baffled expression on his scruffy face. Quack gently washed blood from Sam's round face with a damp towel. "I feel much improved already, my friends," Sam said.

Ace hovered behind Quack. Ironclad groused from the background, "This Smuggler's Crossroads business is a mess and it ain't getting any tidier. Is he ready to make a statement?"

Quack said, "I'd say so. Go ahead, Sam."

Sam closed his eyes. "I paid the cab driver for his services and he drove away. I was a little bit lost, so I looked around and checked street signs until I knew the direction of Mrs. Gemrock's apartment. As I came around a corner, I glimpsed a man with a rat head peering out of a doorway arch. Its pointed nose and beady eyes disturbed me. It was a mask, but its illusion was powerful. I ducked behind a tree to watch and wait."

"Ratface, huh?" Ironclad jotted in his notepad.

"I watched until Mr. Thornby appeared, coming from Mrs. Gemrock's flat. He approached the doorway where the rat-man hid. I should have acted faster. Belatedly, I ran toward them. The rat-man hit Mr. Thornby with a small club, and he fell without a sound. I charged in, for the sight of this injustice filled my heart with a fire of anger."

"Understandable, Sam. Understandable," Quack said.

"There was a second man — a man I did not see at first. I caught a glimpse of him, and then my own head burst into pain. I fell, defeated before I had struck a blow."

Ace said, "And you came straight back here when you could?"

"Yes, Lady Ace. I must have slipped into unconsciousness. I did not hear or see anything more, but when I woke up, I was alone. I persuaded a cab driver to take me here instead of the hospital. I persuaded him with a large tip, which, alas, I could not give him. My wallet is gone."

By next afternoon, quiet and order reigned in the front office of C. Carroway and Associates. The construction was complete. The front office held Mrs. Figgins's reception area and a lounge with lots of windows.

The back wall had a door and a one-way mirror. Behind the mirror lay the observation room. The door, bulletproof, led to storage nooks, the observation room, and the staircase to the fourth floor.

In the front office, Mrs. Figgins had her environment arranged. Behind her desk, she had a couple of hidden buttons to press, in case something came in the door she couldn't handle. But Mrs. Figgins could handle anything.

At the moment, it was a pair of reporters. Sharp newshawks both, the men teamed up in an attempt to get Mrs. Figgins off balance.

"We only want a quick interview!" said one.

"The people have a right to know if Ace Carroway is alive! How they gonna know if nobody sees her?" said the other.

The waspish, straight-backed Mrs. Figgins droned nasally, "Do you have an appointment?"

The reporters were thrown off stride for a split second.

Mrs. Figgins injected into the gap, "No visitors without appointments."

One threw his hands in the air. "Awright, awright! Make me an appointment."

Mrs. Figgins's monotone managed to sound smug, somehow. "No appointments for reporters."

"Oh, come off it! Stop trying to brush us off! The public has a right to know!"

Mrs. Figgins regarded them over her half-moon glasses, blinking once, slowly. "No, actually. But citizens have a right to privacy. No appointments for reporters. Good day, gentlemen."

Bruised by the solidity of the brick wall that was Mrs. Figgins, the frustrated newshawks gave up.

Ace descended from the fourth floor in time to observe the reporters slink away. When it was safe to emerge, she said, "Excellent work, Mrs. Figgins."

"My pleasure, ma'am." Mrs. Figgins gave a tiny, evil smirk.

"Did Sarah Gemrock call back?"

"No, ma'am!"

"All right. I wish she would. She must be beside herself with worry."

"Yes, ma'am."

Ace ducked into the observation room. Tombstone was on watch in the dim space behind the one-way mirror. He slouched with his hat pulled down over his eyes and his cowboy-booted feet propped up on a chair.

He glanced over at Ace's arrival. "Howdy!"

Ace said, "Hi, Tombstone. Is all the radio gear installed?"

"Yep."

"How often do batteries need to be changed in the pulse emitters?"

Tombstone said, "In the roadster? The battery'll last a couple of days, but it's hooked to the alternator, so it'll recharge if the roadster gets driven."

"Good detail to know! We have several directional loop antennas here, and I delivered a couple to the hangar, too."

"Ah think we're all set, then, Ace! Say, look! Here comes that feller, Jeremy Braggs. What's he doing back here again?" Tombstone's bright facial expression drooped in distaste.

The nattily dressed Braggs spoke to Mrs. Figgins, but he could not be heard from inside the soundproofed observation room. He handed her a modest arrangement of daisies and carnations in a vase, and a card. Tombstone leaned forward and flipped a switch built into a small table that supported a telephone. The amplifier's vacuum tubes warmed up in moments.

Mrs. Figgins's voice fuzzed into audibility from intercom speakers set in the ceiling over their heads. " . . . them to her. I'm sure she'll like them very much, Mister Braggs."

"Thank you very much! I do appreciate it, ma'am. Good day to you!" Braggs lifted his hat to Mrs. Figgins and beamed her a smile. He sauntered from the office.

Ace watched his every move very closely.

Tombstone squirmed. "Aw, gee, Ace! What do you see in that guy?"

Ace stood and gazed out toward Mrs. Figgins. "I see a handsome young man, reasonably fit. Virile, even. He's intelligent, with good taste in clothes and excellent, if slightly old-fashioned manners."

"Aw, don't tell me you're gonna go out with 'im?"

"I'm considering it." Ace left the observation room to examine the card and flowers.

Chapter 18

Ace, with flowers, left the C. Carroway and Associates office on foot. She stopped at the Low Dive Café for a bite to eat. The woman in factory coveralls and dark circles under her eyes sat nursing a coffee. Ace presented her with the bouquet of flowers.

"Here. They'll brighten up your table."

"Huh? Well, thanks! Ace, right?" The woman buried her face in the bouquet and inhaled, smiling dreamily.

"Yes, that's right. I didn't catch your name."

"Dolores."

"A pleasure, Dolores." Ace regarded the woman warmly. She spoke toward the counter. "Mom? How about a grilled tomato and cheese and some soup?"

"Comin' up. How ya doin', Ace?" The tattooed mass behind the counter came to life and reached for a spatula.

"I'll pay for that," said a voice from the door.

Mom squinted at the door. "What we got here? Zorro?"

Darryl Dashing stood in the doorway, resplendent in a new scarlet-lined cape and an updated mask with scarlet trim. He carried a single-stem red rose.

"It's a purely social visit, Miss Carroway, I assure you. In fact, I solemnly swear it!" the trim man bowed deeply.

"If you say so," Ace said.

"Oh, this is precious!" gleefully commented Dolores, rocking back in her chair and ogling the costumed character.

Darryl Dashing glanced at Dolores and her full bouquet of flowers, then down at his single stem. He offered the rose to Ace, though his smile faltered and his lower face colored pinker.

"Thank you," Ace said.

"Shall we sit?" Dashing offered, gesturing to a table. He held Ace's chair for her, and called to Mom, "Proprietor! I'll have whatever Miss Carroway is having."

"Sure thing, Zorro," Mom grunted.

Ace wore her wide-belted flight suit. Fashion-wise, she was vastly outdone by the glitzy Darryl Dashing. The swashbuckler settled in across the table from Ace with an artful sweep of his cloak and a roguish grin. He had even, strong teeth, a dimple in his chin, and a shading of brown beard stubble on his pale face. The effect was quite striking. Certainly, Dolores's eyes never left the dashing rogue.

"I have to ask. Why the mask?" Ace inquired.

"I simply wish to be anonymous, that's all. I have nothing to hide, otherwise."

"So Darryl Dashing isn't your real name." Ace said with a wry twist of her lips.

"No. And yet, I abhor deception. Ironic, is it not?"

Moving quietly for a man of his mass, Mom suddenly loomed by the table. He dished out two bowls of split pea soup and two plates with hot grilled sandwiches, garnished with dill pickle wedges. "Ya want some coffee?"

"Sure, Mom. Thanks." Ace said, reaching to pat her pockets.

"I said I would pay, Miss Carroway," Darryl Dashing reminded.

"Oh, I remember. You can pick up the tab, I suppose. I'm checking for your watch. Yes, here it is. It stayed in my pocket from yesterday." Ace slid a shiny pocket watch to the table, the one with an ornate baobab tree engraved on the back.

"Oh!" Dashing exclaimed, "Oh, bless you! I've shed real tears over this thing, believe it or not! I thought it was gone forever."

"A sentimental item, I take it?" Ace asked around a nibble of cheese-and-tomato.

"Yes, the Benjamin Society—," Dashing sighed, "I suppose I can't go into detail and still be anonymous. But, yes, this is a sentimental treasure. Thank you, Miss Carroway."

"You're welcome. I'm glad it got back to its owner. So. Not to spoil the broth, but: What should I know about Jeremy Braggs?"

The visible half of Dashing's face flushed for the second time. "Ah, well. I admit it. My theatrics are, well, theatrics. I don't have anything against him. He's probably a sterling citizen. It just makes it easier to appear to be gallant when I have competition."

"Competition for what? I'm not in the market for a companion," Ace said, bluntly.

"Ah, well, a fellow can dream, can't he?" Dashing blushed deeper, then applied himself to the food, with gusto.

Dashing stuck to topics of Broadway plays, literature, music, and the death of chivalry for the rest of the meal. Ace all but gave up on finding out new facts. When she asked, directly, "Why did you set the smoke bomb at the concert hall?" Dashing winked and shook his head from side to side.

When he bowed gallantly and whirled away into the night, Ace sat and spindled a napkin, pursing her lips. Dolores came over, taking the chair Dashing had vacated.

Ace's left eyebrow upticked. She glanced around. Only Dolores and Mom still occupied the room.

"Ace," said Dolores, "you acted pretty tense with that guy."

"Did I?" Ace replied, both eyebrows shooting up. Ace relaxed, "Oh, it's not what you think. He means no harm."

Dolores nodded. "Not what I meant, honey. A picturesque chin dimple like that, bringing you a rose, no less! It makes me wonder if you want any advice about how to handle *men*. How old are you?"

Mom rumbled from behind the counter, "Dolores …"

Dolores raised a hand to ward off any wrath from the mountainous short order cook.

"Sorry, Ace, I'm not prying. Don't give it to me in years, give it to me in experience. You ever been kissed?"

"You *are* pryin'," Mom pointed out.

Ace looked back and forth between them, then sighed. "No."

"Thought so. Intuition," Dolores said, gently. "I guess I just felt all your walls going up."

"Walls?" Ace wondered, "Yes, I guess I have walls.

I'm used to fighting for things. Was I rude?"

"No, no, your momma raised you right," chuckled Dolores. "I can tell you're a scrapper, and I'm here to tell you something that might shock you."

"Skip the preamble, Thomas 'Dolores' Jefferson," Mom grumped.

"Shock me? Should I ground myself?" Ace smirked.

Dolores ignored the hecklers. She blazed with sudden passion, locking eyes with Ace. "You keep those walls up! You keep fighting! I'm glad you were nervous, because you can't trust a man on the make."

Ace's face melted like soft butter. "Aww. You're taking care of me."

"Well, yeah." Dolores leaned back. "So, you gonna listen?"

"I'm listening, but do you really think he was on the make? I mean, actually interested in me, for me?" Ace's hand strayed to touch her facial scars.

Dolores scrunched up her face. "Hun. Don't go thinking you're ugly or something. Those scars just add interest. You got plenty of what it takes to catch men, if that's what you want."

Ace blinked. "No!"

Dolores nodded. "Thought not. So, how about it? You going to keep fighting? You really can't trust men, and I can back it up with stories."

"I want to hear those stories, some day," Ace replied.

Mom grunted. "For what it's worth, I agree with Dolores. Don't trust 'em an inch."

"It's good advice. I'll take it," Ace said firmly.

97

Chapter 19

Ace craved action more than rest. She needed to chase the clue Darryl Dashing dropped about the Benjamin Society. She retraced her steps back toward the Carroway agency along sidewalks peppered with single-minded pedestrians, their heads down, their feet clicking purposefully.

Ace's mind drifted back over Dolores's advice. A reminiscent upward curve of her lips drooped to a petulant frown. She protested to herself, "But I can kiss someone without trusting them. It's not like it *means* anything these days. It's 1921, for Pete's sake."

A block away from her destination, a sedan on the street slowed to walking speed and paralleled her.

"What now?" she muttered.

The driver of the brown Oakland leaned over the passenger seat. His handsome face grinned boyishly. Jeremy Braggs said, "Miss Carroway! They're giving balloon rides at Washington Park!"

Ace's eyes widened from suspicious slits to round portals of childlike wonder. "Balloon rides?"

"Come on!" Braggs leaned even farther and opened the passenger door. Ace bounced in. The Oakland accelerated.

Three cars back, a van followed. Bert leaned between Tombstone, the driver, and Gooper, the passenger. His face showed dismay. "She got in?"

Gooper wagged his head from side to side. "Cor!"

Sam was stuck behind Bert. He tried to see past the

lawyer, first to the left, then to the right. "I dislike this."

Tombstone shifted gears, staying well back. "Ah agree. It smells like the north end of a southbound Longhorn."

Quack was absent because of Hamlet.

The sour quartet followed the brown Oakland to Washington Park. The Oakland pulled to the curb near the archway, famous for its George Washington sculptures. Tombstone hurriedly parked as well, behind a delivery truck.

Sam said, "I suppose we follow on foot, now, sahibs. Lady Ace, she is possessed of sharp eyes. We must be careful, lest we be discovered."

Gooper said, "Oi've got a pair o' field glasses."

Bert said, "Lose the Stetson, Tombstone."

The quartet piled out of the van and ran under some park trees. In the deepening gloom of twilight, they were effectively invisible. All the light pooled in the main plaza, where a platform had been erected around a gas-fed flame. In the air, but tethered by a sturdy rope, was a garishly painted balloon.

As the men watched Ace and Braggs stroll toward the platform, attendants winched the balloon out of the air and back to the platform. Hands reached for the large basket underneath, in which a man and a woman stood waving. Brawny arms affixed the mouth of the balloon over the flame, to be refilled with hot air.

A man in a straw hat distantly barked, "Take flight in our famous Montpelier! Five minutes, five dollars!"

Gooper trained his field glasses on the pair.

"They're just walking."

Bert said, "Well, at least it's a public place and not some dark alley. That makes me feel a little better."

Sam said, "Ah! It is the balloon. He lured her with the promise of a balloon ride!"

Tombstone said, "Good thinkin', pardner."

"Tombstone," Bert said, slowly. "Do you have a rifle in the van?"

"Shore! I got me a trusty li'l firestick in the back."

"Get it. Just in case."

Tombstone grumbled, "In case o' what?" But he ambled back to the van to get his long-range hunting rifle. On the plaza, the crowd of people slowly thinned with the slow approach of evening. A family with several children tossed pinches of bread to hundreds of gluttonous pigeons.

When Tombstone returned, Gooper reported, "Braggs paid for a ride. They're next in line. The libidinous lothario's got his arm around her waist. Ace is all smiles."

The faces of the four pinched as if they had discovered worms in their apples.

"Ding-nab it!" Tombstone said. "Now I got a rifle, an' all I can think of is using it. On him."

"Our hatred of him seems irrational," said Sam. "Why do we distrust him so?"

Bert said, "How can you trust anyone better looking than me?"

Tombstone said, "I *don't* trust ya."

"Exactly my point."

None seemed able to improve upon that answer. They watched Ace scissor into the basket of the balloon, ignoring about six helping hands ready to assist her, including those of Braggs.

Gooper reported, "Cheeky grin, Ace 'as."

Sam said, "They launch!"

Levers released, and the gas bag leapt into the air, sweeping the basket along. The ground crew let the capstan spin, and the tether lengthened as the balloon climbed high. The remnants of the crowd murmured, and a few people clapped. The pigeons chased breadcrumbs, immune to the spectacle.

Gooper's teeth clenched. "He put his arm around 'er again. He's whisperin' them sweet nothings in 'er ear. Me friends, Oi'm startin' tew panic."

Bert said, "Ace! C'mon! You're worth about twenty-nine million of him."

"She hain't listenin', Bert," Gooper said. "'E's hypnotized her or somethin'. Their lips are getting close."

Sam said, "Oh. Oh, my. How close is that?"

Gooper said, "Too close. I can almost count down. Three. Two. Ow!"

A rifle spoke sharply in the cool twilight. The entire park full of pigeons took startled flight.

"Tombstone!" Sam scolded.

Tombstone lowered his rifle. "Oops."

Gooper grinned, then hastily raised his field glasses. "They're looking around. No kissin'."

Bert said, "The ground crew's reeling in the tether. Maybe early, maybe on time. I can't tel."

Sam said, "I see a policeman, sahibs. His facial expression is, shall we say, wrathful."

Chapter 20

The associates beat a hasty retreat to the van and thus evaded an encounter with the irritated officer. They managed to observe Ace and Braggs part ways. Braggs drove off in his Oakland. Ace jogged away southward.

The next morning, Tombstone ambled up to the lab with his rifle. Placidly, he cleaned the barrel and the action. During the process Ace breezed past the open door. A moment later, her head and shoulders reappeared, tilting in for a second look. Her lips compressed.

Tombstone grinned big. "Howdy, ma'am!"

Ace opened her mouth as if to say something, but closed it and gave her head a negative shake. She disappeared.

Shortly, she left the office altogether, saying, "I'm pursuing a clue at the library."

When a rumpled Quack meandered into the reception area, eyes blinking owlishly, the associates shoved a cup of coffee into his hands and filled him in on the previous evening's scandals.

He said, "I know we want to protect Ace, but, really, kisses aren't harmful."

"Spoken like an actor," Bert replied in withering tones.

Quack said, nose in the air, "Oh, you're one to talk, mister pucker lips. Actors may stage-kiss as required by the script, but you'll kiss anything wearing a skirt."

"Not so! I have excellent taste in women. I'm very particular. Mayhap you are envious of my success, oh dateless one."

"Ow, put a sock in it, yew two!" Gooper said.

Sam said, "Yes, please. We have these smuggling reports to read."

Ace returned by afternoon. Tombstone briefed everyone on how to operate the teletype machine. After the lesson, Quack excused himself from further action. "It's the final few days before opening night. I'd better concentrate on *Hamlet*. Sorry, everybody."

There was a general chorus of sympathy and forgiveness until Quack's hangdog facial expression brightened. They all followed him down to the door, wishing him well in his thespian endeavors.

"I'm all warmed up inside," he said. "Thanks, everybody." Quack left, head high.

The front office phone rang.

"Carroway and Associates, Investigations," said Mrs. Figgins. There was a pause. "I'll see if she's in, Mister Braggs."

Mrs. Figgins peered over her half-moon glasses at Ace, eyebrows raised.

Ace hesitantly took the phone from Mrs. Figgins.

"Good afternoon, Mr. Braggs. Cecilia Carroway, here."

The four men milled around, ostensibly walking back to the fourth floor. But they stretched out the task of placing one foot in front of the other for such a long time that they overheard the rest of what Ace was saying. Even the scorching schoolmarm glare cast upon them by Mrs. Figgins didn't much speed them up.

"The Café Charles? Well … All right. Six o'clock. Until then, Mr. Braggs." Ace hung up. She faced the shuffling row of amateur gossips and put her fists on her hips. Her lips compressed to a flat line. "Fellas, is there something I should know?"

They exchanged sheepish glances. Eventually, Bert said, "There's something about him."

Tombstone nodded feverishly. "We don't trust the varmint."

"Come here. I want to tell you a few things." She stepped to the lounge area by the windows.

The men shuffled over.

Ace said, "There's something fishy about all this, agreed?"

"Yep!"

"Yes, memsahib."

"Aye!"

"For sure!"

Ace said, "Did anyone pick up that Darryl Dashing and Jeremy Braggs are working together?"

"Huh?"

"No!"

"Wot?"

"Yes, I suspected so," Sam told his feet.

Ace said, "What did you notice, Sam?"

Sam stroked his curled mustache. "On the night of the climb up the building and over the roof, the Dashing man jumped down a slide. The Braggs man put his hands out, to stop anyone from jumping after. I thought his gesture came too quickly. No one yet understood that the slide had broken into two pieces, and that to jump would be death. It was gloomy and hard to see."

Ace nodded. "Very good. I noticed that, too. I also happened to notice on the second encounter involving the fencing sabre, that Braggs had recently burned his thumb. The small oval wound could easily have come from exposure to a welding torch, and the welds under the manhole cover were also recent. I do not think Darryl Dashing knows how to operate a welding torch. His hands are those of an accountant or stenographer."

Ace glanced toward Gooper. "I spent a productive hour at the library this morning. The baobab symbol belongs to a particular botanical conservancy group called the Benjamin Society."

Gooper blinked. "Oh! Crikey, yeh. I should'ha remembered them. They preserve wild plants."

"Correct," Ace said. "They take donations, and give back tokens of gratitude. The bigger the donation, the more expensive the gift. I believe the engraved pocket watch is one such inducement. It stands to reason that Darryl Dashing is a donor."

"A noble gesture," said Gooper.

Bert groused, "Not so fast. He's a case. Crying 'fire' in a theater full of people is lunatic!"

Tombstone said, "Saving kittens. Returning stolen purses. Havin' his picture in the newspaper. Yep, I'd say we got him pegged. He's an attention-grabbing do-gooder."

Ace continued, "On the other hand, Jeremy Braggs gives fewer clues. He is very careful with himself. Perhaps he is a closet do-gooder, too, as Tombstone puts it. Maybe there's a whole club of them."

Sam shook his head from side to side. "Logically, Lady Ace, his interest in you is no such thing."

Ace did not have an answer, unless it was that the golden tones of her face deepened in a flush.

An hour later, as the four men lounged in the observation room, a middle aged woman came in. Her dress was neat, and her accessories tasteful, but she had dark circles under her eyes. She wore a splint on two fingers of one hand.

Tombstone reached to flick on the amplifier. Mrs. Figgins assured the visitor, "Miss Carroway has been trying to reach you. I'm sure she'll be happy you stopped by. One moment, Mrs. Gemrock." Mrs. Figgins reached for her telephone and dialed.

Sarah Gemrock drifted toward the lounge as Mrs. Figgins spoke into her telephone. "Mrs. Gemrock to see you, Miss Carroway." Mrs. Figgins told the visitor, "She'll be right down." She hung up and went back to her typing.

Bert frowned at Mrs. Figgins through the one-way glass. "Is she typing agency business, or is she writing a novel?"

Sam said, "Shh!"

"But the room is soundproofed," Bert said, "We can talk at normal volume and not be heard out there."

Tombstone said, "That ain't what Sam meant, Bert."

Ace descended from the fourth floor. She jogged to Sarah Gemrock and the two embraced.

"Sarah, I'm glad to see you. Any news about Cheswick?"

"I'm afraid not. Not even a ransom note. I don't understand it."

Ace took Sarah's hand. "I have a theory. It's not a comforting one, though."

"It has to be better than not knowing! Tell me."

"All right. Cheswick is a chemist, and he worked in Bavaria before the Great War. In particular, he worked on gases, one of which was chlorine. The Ottomans tried to absorb him into their war machine, but he ran away. I assume you know all that?"

"I knew. I also know it is the cause of the haunted look he sometimes gets in his eyes. He injured his own ear when some gas bottles leaked. In his bleakest moods, he blames himself for the gas attacks during the war!"

Ace frowned. "He should not. The mastermind was Darko Dor."

"That's what I tell him. He needs to hear it often. Poor, sensitive man."

"My educated guess is that Cheswick was kidnapped on the orders of Darko Dor."

"What? Darko Dor is alive? But why? Why would he kidnap Cheswick?"

"The only thing that makes sense is that Darko Dor is back to making weapons, including chemical weapons," Ace said grimly. "He is trying to conscript Cheswick Thornby."

"Oh!" Sarah put a hand to her mouth. Her eyes became watery. "But Cheswick would never work for that monster!"

"I agree."

"Oh, this is the worst!"

"Not quite. The United States is hot for Darko Dor right now. His face is on posters from Hoboken to Sedona. Since he can't be here in person, he has to work through middlemen. Does the name Smuggler's Crossroads ring a bell?"

"No."

"No reason it should. But it gives us a little bit of time. If we can find Smuggler's Crossroads soon enough, maybe we can save Cheswick before he's shipped overseas."

Sarah had grown paler than when she came in. "It seems a faint hope."

"But hope, nevertheless. Does the name Gristle mean anything to you?"

"No."

"Futa?"

"No."

"Ratface?"

"Well, he was the one that robbed me and broke my finger, wasn't he? He laughed, you know. He laughed as he beat me to the ground." Sarah shuddered.

"I'm so sorry, Sarah!" Ace said, putting an arm around Sarah's shoulders.

"There is true evil in this world, Cecilia! That Ratface man is proof of it. He's a devil! Do you know he also stole the box of chocolates that Cheswick had given me that very evening?"

Ace froze.

Sarah peered at her. "What is it?"

Ace said, in a choked-off voice, "Belmont chocolates? What color was the tag?"

"Yes, Belmont. The tag was yellow. My dear! You're trembling!"

Ace said, "Oh, I'm trembling all right! I've never been so angry! Devil, you said, and a brazen devil at that. Moments after he robbed you, he called the ambulance at my request. All that time, he was holding your chocolate box under his arm! All that time, your money and jewelry were lumps in his pockets!"

Ace leapt up. "And to think I almost kissed him!"

Part Three

The
Handsome Devil

CHAPTER 21

At 5:30, Ace surveyed a ragged row of motley associates. "Well, you were right."

Bert said, "And that's all we needed to hear. Thanks, Ace! So, can we bag him?"

Ace shook her head. "No. It makes even less sense, now. We have to play the game a little longer. But not past tonight. Braggs is Ratface, and Ratface knows all about Smuggler's Crossroads. If we don't learn anything useful by playing along, then, I agree. We should bag him. Or have ONI do it."

"Naw! Us, please!" Gooper said.

Ace laughed. "Did I ever say that I appreciate you fellas? Well, I do."

"Even me?" asked Tombstone, his face drooping like a doleful basset hound.

"Yes, Tombstone. Especially you. I was in mid-air, and he was warm and so—" Ace broke off, flushed. "Never mind. The trouble with his charm is that he turns it on and off."

Bert said, "I take it we're following you to Café Charles?"

"Yes, Bert! The four of you will shadow me. You know about our trackable pulse transmitters. I will wear one under my belt." Ace tapped her chin with a finger. "I'd better take the roadster. It will raise suspicion if I don't. You can take Bert's car. Right, Bert? Take a loop antennae so you can track the pulse transmitter."

Ace drove the few blocks to the Café Charles in a low, large-engined four door roadster discreetly equipped with extra radio gear. Jeremy Braggs waited in a natty pinstripe suit and hat. He opened the car door for Ace's exit and showed a surge of animated admiration.

"Gracious! That is a magnificent set of wheels, Miss Carroway! That engine must really thunder. I bet it's comfortable inside. Is that leather upholstery? Ah, but I forget myself. Come, Miss Carroway, we have a table under the awning out on the sidewalk. Thank you for meeting with me."

They settled in at the table amid other customers, with passers by within arm's reach on the other side of a low rope fence. The weather was brisk. Ace wore her usual flight suit with wide belt.

"The balloon ride last night was quite thrilling. And the flowers were lovely."

"I am glad you enjoyed them! Beautiful flowers for a beautiful— Ah, but forgive me! That just slipped out."

"Are you sure, Mr. Braggs? You don't seem the type to let words slip when you don't mean them to."

Braggs cleared his throat and straightened his tie. "I wish not to be a cad, Miss Carroway. I have only the highest regard for you, and my intentions are entirely honorable, I assure you."

"I'm not sure whether to be pleased or disappoint-ed." Ace's seat refused to become comfortable. She squirmed.

A fleeting wolfish smile curved Braggs's lips. "I'm an open book, Miss Carroway. Ask me what you will."

"All right. What do you do for a living?"

"I'm in construction. I assist an architect at building sites."

His polished poise seemed impenetrable. It stood to reason that small talk could not break the stalemate, but what about something outrageous? Ace made her voice as casual and innocent as she could.

"Have you ever heard of Smuggler's Crossroads?"

There was a brief flicker in Braggs's eyes. A widen-ing of his irises. But he swept the momentary reaction away with a dismissive hand gesture. "Why, no! It sounds adventuresome, though, whatever it is."

The coffee arrived, interrupting the conversation. When the waiter had gone, dapper Braggs leaned for-ward and said in low tones, "I am concerned about the Dashing fellow. I've seen him lurking about. Twice now. I think he has it in for me."

"Oh? Do you know him from before? Before the incident at the concert hall, I mean."

"No. I had never clapped eyes on him before that night. I wonder if he's mentally stable! Say, I never thought of that! He might just be off his rocker."

"I suppose it's a possibility," said Ace agreeably.

As they talked, Darryl Dashing himself entered Ace's peripheral vision, mask and all. The swashbuck-ler approached on tiptoe behind Braggs, equipped with a canister fire extinguisher, the type filled with water and pressurized air.

Ace was willing to bet the device was pumped up and ready to gush. She kept her eyes focused on Braggs. "He gets under your skin, maybe? Makes you mad?"

"I'll say! I mean, yes, I have to admit, he makes me see red, especially when he was raving about sweeping you off your feet. I bet he set that fire himself."

"You'd probably be quite livid if he were here and about to pounce on us again, then?"

"Why, yes! Of course I—" Braggs's eyes widened at Ace's amused tones, and he spun around in his chair. Dashing's timing was perfect; his jet of water struck Braggs full in the face

Dashing cackled, "No one escapes the masked eyes of the all-seeing Darryl Dashing! Fade away, you faker! You have lost at every turn!"

Nearby patrons shrieked and shouted. The nearest bolted out of their chairs. Ace stood, ignoring the water splatters striking her flight suit.

"Clown! Buffoon! This is the last straw!" Braggs shouted. He leapt up and gave chase.

Hooting merrily, Darryl Dashing played hare, running at full speed. Braggs played hound, leaping the low barrier of the sidewalk café and baying. Ace loped along after the pair, shaking her head in wonderment.

The chase was longer than the average Ace had come to expect. It was two and a half blocks away from the New York bustle before they cut into a lonely alley. It was a cluttered dead end. A delivery truck sat in the *cul de sac*, inert and forlorn. Stubby walls, low staircases for back doors, dumpsters, and trash cans crowded the alley.

Darryl Dashing, huffing and gasping from exertion, circled around to the back of the delivery truck and disappeared. The truck rocked as he got in. Jeremy Braggs followed.

Ace slowed down. She expected an explosion of shouting and fisticuffs blows. She heard nothing.

Her forehead furrowed. She stopped and stared at the silent truck. The back of her neck prickled, and she whipped around toward the alley entrance. From behind the alley's obstacles a half circle of four moth-eaten figures stepped into view.

Each hard face held blank, uncaring eyes. Each scarred fist held a snub-nosed pistol. All the pistols pointed at Ace.

CHAPTER 22

Jeremy Braggs appeared, with a fifth thug trailing behind him. Braggs had a club in his hand. The ease with which he swung it indicated considerable experience with the weapon.

Slapping the club into his open palm, Braggs spoke a few words. His accents changed, now more at home in a seedy dive than a concert hall.

"Sorry, doll. You'll come out all right if you play nice, but right now, I need to you turn around and face the boys, there. Turn around. Go on. The alternative ain't pretty."

Ace racked her brain to invent methods of escape, but all her odds calculations summed up to bullet holes. Resistant as a rusty bolt, she followed directions and slowly rotated. Braggs left her field of vision and became ominously invisible behind her.

Tense and hyper alert, Ace felt the expected air motions on the skin of her scalp. For a split second the touch of the descending club sent vibrations down a few hairs. With catlike reflexes, she snapped her head downward to try to match the speed of the club.

It wasn't enough. A clunk sounded and stars exploded through her vision. She crumpled unceremoniously to the ground and lay still.

But she wasn't unconscious. She mentally recited a *Wing Chun* mantra and calmed her breathing and heart, keeping her eyes closed and her body relaxed.

She heard Braggs chuckle, but the sound was chilling, not funny.

She heard running footsteps and the excited voice of Darryl Dashing. "No! By heavens, what are you do-ing? Braggs, you devil! You never said —!"

But Dashing's new oratory cut off. Braggs growled, "Oh, shaddap!" A hollow clunk sounded. A second body heavily slithered to the grimy alley cobblestones.

"Right," Braggs said. "Let me just get some keys …." Ace felt hands paw at her, and reach down her zippered knee pocket where she kept the keys to the roadster. Ace went deep into her mantra. With great effort, she controlled her revulsion and kept still.

The hand slipped out of her pocket. The keys jin-gled.

"Awright. Load 'em both up. Take 'em to the warehouse. I'll meet you there, shortly, an' then it's payday. Savvy?"

"Right, boss!" said a gravelly voice.

Rough hands gripped Ace at armpits and ankles. Men grunted as she felt herself lifted and hauled. The smell of unwashed bodies assaulted her nose.

They carried her swinging body up a creaky loading ramp and into the delivery truck. Hastily and roughly, they dumped her on its metal floor. Ace's head throbbed, and she saw stars again.

They tossed Dashing's body half on top of hers. The crude men slid the ramp in, then climbed in and shut themselves in the cargo area of the van. Ace sensed there were three in the back and two in the front.

She again calculated probabilities regarding five

thugs with guns. She decided to keep playing dead.

CHAPTER 23

The truck rumbled and jostled for half an hour. Its suspension did nothing to dull the knocks of pavement cracks and potholes. Ace silently bore the steady accumulation of bruises.

The three pistol-packing men sat mute in the dark box for fifteen minutes. For half a minute they grumbled worries about getting paid. Their words did nothing to illuminate where they were going or why.

Ace's headache dulled to a mere throbbing. Dashing began to moan and stir. The truck lurched to a halt and the engine rattled down to silence.

"Awright, get 'em in the cage," the gravelly voice said. Bangs and metallic scrapes signaled doors opening and the reattachment of the ramp.

Ace emulated the moaning Darryl Dashing and squirmed as if delirious. The gangsters seized her upper arms. She pretended to half support herself as they dragged her from the truck. Ace's slitted eyes glimpsed a lonely warehouse with only trees nearby. No other buildings were visible.

Inside, haphazard stacks of crates leaned in disorder. Dangling, glaring electric light bulbs illuminated small patches but left large areas in shadow. In a corner cleared of crates lay a steel cage.

The men dragged Ace and Dashing inside and dropped them in heaps. The door clanged shut. Keys rattled and clanked, and the lock snicked shut.

The men tucked their guns out of sight and grumbled. "Awright. We did our part. Where's mister moneybags?"

No one knew.

One squint-eyed fellow in a cap suggested, "Finish our poker game?" The five scooted out of sight behind some stacks of crates.

Uncoiling fluidly, Ace rose and examined the cage. The bars were so thick, she wondered if it was a bear cage. It was welded in sections a dozen bars wide, and each section bolted to the next.

She glanced toward the area where the poker game was starting. No one. The door they had entered by was out of sight, too.

Without fanfare, Ace slipped a small adjustable wrench from underneath her wide belt and began disassembling a section of the cage.

"Wh- where are we?" moaned a voice.

Ace glanced down at Darryl Dashing, who rubbed his head, peering at Ace foggily.

"Shhh!" she murmured, much more quietly than his moan. "I'm not sure. Fifteen miles upstate of New York, in a warehouse. Now, keep your voice low. Tell me your name. Your real name, please."

Ace worked slowly, deliberately, and very quietly lest she make clanks that would attract attention from the poker-playing thugs. She removed one nut and washer and dropped them in a thigh pocket. She went on to the next.

Dashing was trembling slightly. He still had his mask on. "Oh, my aching head! My name is Durbin Dwynt and I've been a fool!"

"A bit," Ace agreed. "Did you do it for money?"

"Right on the first try, Miss Carroway. He told me he wanted to catch your eye. He wanted my help so he could be seen as your protector. I was down on funds, so I agreed to help."

Durbin Dwynt squinted at Ace, trying to bring his farsighted eyes into focus. "I didn't act my part well. I was supposed to be rough to you, but when it came time, I couldn't bring myself to do it."

"If you had, I would have pressed assault charges."

"Oh. Oh, my. Jail? I would have been mortified. You don't need protecting, Miss Carroway. I can see that, now."

"Durbin. Please get on your hands and knees, right here. I need a boost to reach the ceiling bolts."

"All right," answered the masked man. He acted as a stair step for Ace to undo two bolts at the very top of the cage, sagging a bit under her weight, but gamely holding firm. Ace slipped those bolts completely free and slipped them into her pocket.

"Are we escaping? But those men had guns! My stars!" Durbin's trembling grew, and his voice rose.

Ace hissed, "Shh!"

A voice from beyond the crates said, "Keep it down over there! And for your information, nobody's gonna hear you if you shout, so don't, and if you do, I'll just come over and shoot yer knee cap off, y'hear?"

The rest of the gang coarsely laughed.

A nasal tenor voice said, "Two pair, aces high. Read 'em an' weep!" and then they were back to their game.

Ace stepped off Durbin, much to his relief, and set to work on the bolts in the floor. She strained to loosen them, but they were stubborn.

The outside door handle rattled.

Ace pulled Durbin to the front of the cage and whispered rapidly, "Stand here. It blocks the view of the missing nuts." Ace stood beside him and gripped the bars in gold toned fists.

Jeremy Braggs strutted in, carrying a small cloth bag. He shot a leer toward the cage.

A thug popped his head around the crates. "There you are, Ratface. Finally. What did you do, go sightseeing?"

"A car followed me for a little while. I lost 'em." Braggs sauntered to the poker game and disappeared from view.

His voice accused, "Not watching the prisoners? Amateurs! You don't deserve this. But here it is."

A faint papery plop sound caused coos of appreciation from the thugs.

Braggs said, "You. Count all that out into five equal parts. Everybody else, watch him like a hawk. He's a cheat and a swindler."

"Har! Ain't we all?"

CHAPTER 24

Braggs swaggered over to smirk at Ace and Durbin. Ace stared coolly back. Durbin flushed and balled up his fists.

Braggs grinned big. "Simmer down, tiger. The worst is over. No more bangs on the head, as long as you behave."

"What's this all about, Braggs?" Ace said through tight lips.

"Simple, my dear. You have a choice, and I don't care which you choose. You can be a defiant hero. I'll let you do that. I'm fine with that.

"If you do that, I happen to know a foreign gentleman that wants to buy you off the black market. It's quite a lucrative price. It'll make me rich."

"Darko Dor!" Ace spat.

"Ha! Ha! Right the first time."

"And what's the other choice, just for academic interest?" Ace bit the words off.

"The other choice is — and I find this rather delicious — the other choice is that you pay me the same, and I let you go. I know you've got the dough. You're the heir of Grant Carroway. I bet you've got just canoodles of company stock. I'll be happy to keep you here and write bank letters for you to sign until I've got the cash."

"You're a rat," Ace observed.

"I'm a regular devil!" Braggs said with pride.

"G-got that right!" said Durbin Dwynt.

Another voice broke in. "Hey, Ratface. I mean, mister boss, sir. We got paid. We're outta here, and we never saw your mug. Don't know where 'here' is. Never heard your name. All that."

Braggs sauntered toward the five. "You got that straight. None of this happened. And goodbye. A pleasure doing business."

The five shuffled toward the exit. One rattled the doorknob, out of sight of Ace.

Sudden pandemonium broke loose.

CHAPTER 25

Tombstone's whoops, Gooper's howling, and Bert's and Sam's various exclamations and grunts fell like sweet Chopin on Ace's ears. The vocalizations blended with slaps of fists on flesh and grunts of pain. The melee surged inside the warehouse. Bodies crashed into stacks of crates. Menacing gunshots added to the cacophony.

Ace dove for the two stubborn bolts that were still tight, near the floor of the cage. Blind to the battle near the door, Ace struggled for freedom using her pocket-sized crescent wrench.

"Your men are winning!" blurted Durbin.

Ace could barely hear him over the battle noise.

She claimed victory over one bolt, and banged it out of its hole. "They are outnumbered," Ace said worriedly. She attacked the last nut and bolt with her wrench.

"But most of the crew are already down! Oh! Ouch! Oh! Oh, no!" Durbin gasped in dismay.

Two hollow thunk sounds rang out in rapid succession.

"What? What's happening?" Ace strained at the last, most stubborn nut, her knuckles white, her sinews tight as piano wire.

"Oh!" cried Durbin as another thunk sound rang out, "It's Braggs! Him and his club! He's sapped them all! Everybody's down, now except him and the short one with the mustache."

"Go down, shorty," snarled Braggs.

"Sahib. You should be more polite," Sam's voice came, along with several meaty slap sounds.

Braggs grunted in pain with each blow, and went silent, except for the sound of a boneless body falling to the concrete floor.

Sam panted. "Also, do not leave your solar plexus unguarded."

"Oh! Oh, by golly! Braggs is down!" Durbin said giddily. "I think we won—". He broke off, then moaned. "Oh. Ah. Oh, dear. Oh, my."

There was a series of quiet click sounds, familiar to Ace. Hammers on small, ugly snub-nose pistols were being cocked back.

"Freeze, mister mustache!" grouched the gravelly voice.

"Assuredly, my intimidating gun-wielding friends. I shall not move a muscle."

Ace finally raised her head to view the action. Sam held his hands up, menaced by a clump of gunmen. Braggs lay crumpled on the floor by Sam's feet. Gooper, Tombstone, and Bert stirred as they lay nearby.

Ace did not bother to pocket the last nut and washer. She grasped the bars of the cage section, and pushed out.

The heavy iron grid moved, sounding like a dull bell pelted with rocks. Five bruised ruffians swiveled their heads over. An unnerving sight met their eyes.

The canvas-clad woman with fiery golden eyes strode forth. She accelerated, carrying the section of cage. In one smooth motion she launched the iron grid through the air. The metal grate descended upon them at high velocity and crushing force.

"Aaaaa!" one of the men screeched an instant before the metal landed on top of them. Some pistols fired wildly. At impact, the whole mass mashed to the floor. Arms and legs poked through the bars. The pile of bodies wailed and groaned.

Ace pelted over, wrenched a pistol from one flaccid arm and tossed it away.

Sam recovered nicely, and mirrored Ace, stripping a gun and tossing it away.

But a voice came from the pile. "Nothin' doin' ya dark ape! Step back or the dame gets it!"

Ace and Sam quickly spotted a hand holding a gun steadily at Ace's midsection, and a squint-eyed, desperate face behind it.

Sam and Ace froze. It was knife-edge moment. Death hovered a mere finger-twitch away.

The moment of tense silence was broken by a new gruff voice. "Think again, Charlie. Drop the gun or I'll drop it for you!" An arm thrust a pistol at the head of the crook, the thumb cocking the pistol hammer back.

Ace blinked.

Darryl Dashing held his pistol steady. The eyes in his black mask narrowed. His lips compressed to a thin line modified by the hint of a contemptuous sneer.

The squished thug recalculated. His gun hand went limp.

Sam claimed the thug's gun.

"My hero," Ace said.

In woozy stages, Gooper, Bert, and Tombstone

struggled to their feet and wobbled over to grin down at the flattened criminals.

An engine roar outside interrupted their gloating. Gears clashed. Tires spit gravel.

"Braggs! He's escaping!"

CHAPTER 26

"Let him go. We have to clean house here, for a little while," Ace said.

She pointed at a hefty spool hanging on the wall. "There. Wire." She dug another small tool from her wide belt and handed it to the gangly cowboy. "Here. Wire nippers. Hog-tie 'em. Pack them in the delivery truck."

Tombstone, Sam, Bert, and Gooper sprang to work with gusto. They bound wrists and ankles with great speed but no regard for the comfort of the five gang members, some of whom were still unconscious. The associates dragged the hirelings into the van and arranged them in a repugnant row.

Ace went to the masked Durbin and gingerly removed the gun from his grasp. He surrendered it with a shaky smile.

She said, "Durbin, that was brave, gallant, and, dare I say it? Dashing."

"Th-thanks, milady! I mean, Miss Carroway. My head is splitting. I'm shaking with nerves. But, somehow, I intimidated a ... a real bad guy!" Durbin said in tones of wonder.

"Are you up for driving a truck? I'd like you to deliver these bad bundles to the nearest police station."

"Oh! Yes. Yes, of course. I feel like a million dollars." Durbin puffed his chest out.

"Oh, Durbin?"

"Yes?"

"Before you arrive at the police station, take off the mask. They might get the wrong idea."

Durbin nodded.

Ace grinned at him, then eyed her associates. "Let's let Durbin wow the local constabulary. Are we ready to bag us a Braggs?"

"Yew know it, Ace!" Gooper said. A split lip notched his grin.

"Been chafin' at the bit fer days," Tombstone affirmed.

Bert said, "Time to scratch that itch. Let's go!"

Durbin roared off in the delivery truck. Bert drove his own roadster. Ace sat in front. She picked up the loop antenna and slipped headphones on.

Tombstone smirked with satisfaction. "The roadster has a pinger, too, but Braggs don't know it!"

Ace rotated the loop of wire, listening for the loudest pulse tones. "Sounds like he's heading back to town."

"Who here would like some aspirin?" Sam inquired.

"Me!" simultaneously replied everyone else in the car.

"There's our office." Bert pointed out the obvious as they sailed down Wall Street toward the Old Slip piers.

"Slow down," Ace cautioned Bert. "Keep your eyes peeled," she urged the rest.

"Oy! There!" Gooper stabbed a thick finger to the right.

"Good eye, Gooper!" In the heat of the moment, Tombstone forgot himself and complimented the Brit.

The roadster sat parked twenty yards down a narrow alley, blocking it. All was dark. Bert shut off his lights, killed his motor, and rolled in behind the roadster.

The car stopped. Everyone listened. Only late evening New York traffic noise met their straining ears.

"He can't be more than three minutes ahead of us," Ace murmured. "Pile out, fellas. Keep your eyes peeled. We'll search down this alley first, then neighboring ones."

They raided electric torches from the empty roadster.

"'E left it unlocked, but 'e took the keys," Gooper growled. The associates fanned out, searching the alley.

"Sam, do you think Braggs was bleeding after you finished with him?" Ace asked.

"It is hard to know, Lady Ace. Surely, certain of his facial features were not as regular, afterward."

Tombstone chuckled. "Sam, yer a wonder!"

"I see no blood," Ace sighed. "Or footprints. The pavement is too dry."

"Next alley?" Bert wondered.

"We'd better git along, Ah'm thinkin'," Tombstone said.

"Wait," Ace said. She was watching Gooper and Sam. Gooper was examining a low hole in the alley wall, shining his torch in. "What do you see, Gooper?"

"Erm. An 'ole in the wall." Gooper said, as if announcing something of great significance. He amplified, "Made by some member of genus *Rattus*, without a doubt. Oi'm noticin', though, the 'ole slopes downwards. But I don't think this building 'as any basement."

"Ole?" Bert asked in an aside to Tombstone.

Tombstone translated, "He means hole. Londoners cain't talk right."

"Gooper?" Sam inquired from three steps away, in the middle of the alley. "Pardon me, but can you help me lift this manhole cover?"

Sam wore an apologetic expression. "I have observed that the cover is too clean. Rains should have washed a small amount of sediment on top, but there is none."

Gooper helped Sam wrestle the metal lid out. Everyone beamed electric torches down. Metal ladder rungs led to a flat landing. Concrete steps descended from there in the direction pointed to by the rat hole.

"That's no storm drain or sewer." Bert said.

Ace said, with subdued triumph, "Good job, you two. Let's go. Quietly." Ace leapt down, landed lightly, and descended the steps.

The rest scrambled down and followed. Ace flicked off her torch and whispered, "Lights off!"

The men's torches flicked out.

The passageway sloped downwards and twisted, first to the right and then to the left. It ran along the corner of a building foundation exposed on their left-hand side. The rough walls felt moist, and a smell of mildew wrinkled the nose. With the torches off, their eyes adjusted to see a glow ahead of them. Further-more, they heard voices echoing eerily in the damp, cave-like space.

A slow, ponderous, rolling basso with Japanese accents said, "All right. You are on the list. But you cannot enter for another hour. We cannot afford to have even one person followed."

"None of that, now. Come on. This is an emergency," reverberated the voice of Jeremy Braggs. He bit his words off, tense as a tightrope walker. "Here. Here, I got a little something for ya, Futa."

The Carroway party crept closer and closer, keeping their footfalls quieter than the echoing voices. There was a turn ahead, beyond which a brighter light burned. Ace, foremost, showed as a black silhouette. She slowed at the corner, and eased her eye out to peek.

The ponderous voice purred like a smug cat. "Futa appreciates your generosity, Mister Ratface. You may come in."

Loud metallic scrapes and clangs rang in the tunnel, conjuring images of heavy metal bolts slamming open. Ace crouched lower, like a sprinter at the starting blocks. Her hand motioned to those behind her to come forward.

"Thank you, Futa. Don't worry. I wasn't followed."

Ace held her pose for a split second longer, then, in a flash, she was gone. Her associates hurried after. They rounded the corner to see Ace dart at a closing door.

The foot-thick metal slab weighed at least half a ton. Ace dove into the narrowing crack. Like metal jaws, it closed upon her. It crunched. Ace whimpered, her body sagging.

"Ace!" Tombstone cried.

CHAPTER 27

Ace gasped for air, pushing fruitlessly at the door. Her crushed body prevented the massive door from closing completely.

Suddenly, the door opened. Ace staggered, barely staying on her feet. Beyond her, a behemoth of a man filled the passageway.

Seven feet tall and seemingly seven feet wide, he eyed Ace with wonder and surprise. He thrust out a hog-sized arm and shoved her. He seemed to spend little effort, but Ace catapulted back out into the tunnel. She collided with onrushing Bert and Sam, and they all three went down in a tangle of limbs.

"I think Mister Ratface was followed, after all," Futa said. He shook his head and black topknot in philosophical disapproval. He stepped back out of sight and heaved the vault like door shut.

"Keep the door open!" wheezed Ace.

Tombstone hurled an electric torch at the closing door crack. It wedged in, then splintered into pieces. The door bounced, but resumed its inexorable closing.

Gooper hit the door at full rugby speed. The door popped back open, slamming into the giant guard. Futa staggered back, one hand clapped over his lower face. He dropped the hand, revealing a nosebleed in full flow. He glared at Gooper.

"You are not on the list." He smashed at the British

biologist with a fist.

"Story o' me life!" Gooper retorted. He ducked. He absorbed the titanic force of Futa's blow across his shoulders. It staggered Gooper backwards.

Futa stretched both hands out to push Gooper, but Gooper found footing and launched himself fist first between the giant's hands.

The punch connected, with all Gooper's weight behind it.

Futa's head snapped back, then lolled forward drunkenly. The associates rushed *en masse*, Tombstone leading the charge. They bowled Futa over backwards. Gooper kneeled on the door warden's chest and peered at his face, but the giant seemed dazed.

"That's one scrum yew lost, guv."

Ace came last, upright but holding her ribs. She stepped over the mound of Futa's body and knelt. She reached for Futa's neck and sank her fingers deep into the flesh. After a moment, Futa's unseeing eyes closed altogether.

Ace glanced at her companions. "Carotid artery compression. Cuts oxygen to the brain. He'll sleep a good, long while."

Past the gigantic Futa and lit by a single naked light bulb dangling from the rocky ceiling, a widened portion of the tunnel held a rack of tommy guns and a crate of grenades. The associates looked at the guns and at each other incredulously.

Tombstone whispered, "Where th' heck are we?

New York ain't no war zone!'"

Ace still wheezed after being a nut in a nutcracker. "Definitely Smuggler's Crossroads. We've heard mention of Futa the sumo door warden, remember? Braggs seeks refuge."

Gooper said, ominously, "A nest o' 'uman *Viperidae*."

Tombstone said, "Ya mean nest of vipers? If so, Ah agree, pardner."

"And at least one human rat," Sam said.

Bert pointed to the row of tommy guns. "There's an empty space in the gun rack. I bet Braggs took a machine gun. Expect bullets."

"Are you able to continue, Lady Ace? You were caught between hammer and anvil." Sam whispered.

"I'm all right. Let's go. It might get rougher from here."

In unspoken agreement, they each unhitched a tommy gun from the rack. They delved deeper into the dark den, footfalls silent, speaking no word.

Braggs's voice drifted from further down the tunnel, an octave higher than a minute ago, warbling on the edge of hysteria. "Lower the ceiling! Do it! I don't know if Futa stopped them or not!"

The party approached the end of the tunnel. It pierced raggedly through a foundation wall and opened out into a lighted underground room. The slice of room they could see resembled a portion of a posh lawyer's office. Carpet, leather chairs, desks, and a divan occupied the middle of the room. The walls and ceiling, in contrast, were crumbling concrete and steel girders.

"He better have," answered a bass Jersey voice.

"I'll go see," said a Midwestern tenor.

A broad-shouldered man with suspenders under his disheveled suit jacket lumbered into view. He stopped short and gaped. A crowd packed the tunnel, creeping forward. It did not escape his notice that, among the unsympathetic faces, a half-dozen tommy gun muzzles pointed straight at him. The man reversed course.

"Give up. We've got a small army, here," Bert called sharply, "Lay down your guns, and no one will get hurt."

The man in suspenders ducked back into the room. "Run for it!" he screeched.

"Shoot to wound," Ace said. "Go!"

"Shoot to wound *who*?" Sam was a novice with guns.

The party charged into the "office" in time to see the man with suspenders scurry toward a doorlike rectangle at the far side. Desks with telephones, file cabinets, and office furniture cluttered the underground room.

Tombstone triggered a quick burst of bullets from his gun. The fleeing man let out a howl and crashed to the floor, holding his leg.

"Take care of him, Sam," Ace said. She and the others sprinted over the squirming injured man through the door.

The next room was a jumble of crates and shelves piled with fur pelts, lingerie, paintings, jewelry, fine china, and expensive glass. They caught sight of Braggs, running as if pursued by demons, a tommy gun clutched in his right hand. A blocky hatless fellow was close at his heels. The pair raced around a trio of cages sized for humans and through an archway exit.

Inside the middle cage, a haggard figure in torn trousers and shirtsleeves gasped. He scuttled back in fear.

Ace and her associates could spare no time for the prisoner as they pounded after Braggs and the other. They leapt over and around the piles of valuables and careened around the cages and through the arch, stumbling over rails. The parallel pair of iron rails receded into the gloom of a bare tunnel.

"A railroad?" panted Bert.

"Block 'em wid da car!" barked the Jersey voice from somewhere ahead in the darkness.

"Careful, it's dark in—" Ace's warning was cut off by muzzle flashes and a deep rumble sound. The tunnel filled with echoes of pistol shots.

Gooper gave a howl. "Lumme! Oi've been lacerated!"

The rumble grew louder. A wooden wall emerged from the gloom, spanning the width of the tunnel and growing in size as it approached. It resolved into a heavy, wheeled cart, running on the rails like a mining cart. There was no room around it.

"Tarnation! Head fer th' hills!" Tombstone backpedaled.

CHAPTER 28

Chaotically, Ace, Bert, Gooper, and Tombstone reversed. The heavy rail cart rolled at their heels. They skidded back into the room and scattered left and right. The cart hit the end of its track with a boom, tipping forward onto its front.

Tombstone reversed again. Crouching around the corner, he fired his tommy gun down the tunnel.

"Gaa!" bellowed the Jersey voice.

Gooper clutched a bleeding arm.

Ace glanced, then glanced again at the prisoner in the middle cage. He stood in dignified anxiety. His graying hair, damaged ear, and face Ace recognized.

"Cheswick Thornby!"

Thornby's jaw dropped. "Ace Carroway! Bless my soul!"

Ace spun to the injured Cockney. "Gooper, stay. Bandage your arm and try to get Thornby out of there."

She motioned to Tombstone and Bert and headed back into the rail cart tunnel. The trio raced into the darkness on tiptoes.

No bullets met them. A shadowy blob on the floor rolled back and forth and whimpered in agony. From the gloom beyond the injured smuggler tense voices arose.

"Instructions, bub. Seal it off if it's breached!" grated a new voice, nasal and officious.

"Don't you dare! That's the only way out!" Braggs snarled.

There was a snick sound, and a clunk, and a new rumble began.

"Too late, Ratface!" sneered the nasal voice.

"Noooo!" screamed Braggs.

A continuous barrage of tommy gun fire erupted from a section of tunnel further on. The muzzle flashes strobe lit a grisly vision. Braggs stood, firing the weapon into the crumpling body of a man. The body twisted and contorted as it was pierced over and over by the murderous, point-blank onslaught of bullets. A few hefty levers and gears stuck out from an alcove nearby.

The ceiling beyond the two men appeared to be sliding down, a giant block of descending concrete. Braggs noticed this, too. He kept his finger on the trigger to give himself intermittent light and pelted off in that direction. Ducking his head, he evaded the crushing block and ran on.

In the sudden darkness, amid the rumble of the lowering ceiling, Ace said, "Call ONI."

The rumble ended in a boom. The roll of the artificial thunder echoed and re-echoed, dying away.

"Call 'em how?" Tombstone wanted to know.

"Hey, weren't there telephones back in that first room?" Bert queried.

No one replied.

"Ace?"

Silence.

CHAPTER 29

The man in suspenders lolled on the floor by the human-sized cages and hugged his injured leg. Bert stood watch over him. He counted on his fingers. "Two smugglers injured, one asleep, one dead, one escaped. Ace disappeared into thin air, escape tunnel blocked by a gigantic concrete mass. Is that about right?"

"Oi took a bullet in the arm?" Gooper said. His mind was elsewhere: One by one, he tried keys in the keyhole of Thornby's cage. They had frisked the keyring from the injured thug in suspenders.

"And one chemist rescued, hopefully," Thornby said with a quaver in his voice.

Tombstone emerged from the tunnel, supporting a woozy gangster with wet red leaks on his shoulder, arm, and chest. The cowboy reported, "That last guy is dead. Very dead. Good thing it's dark in there. Ah don't want t' see him any better."

Gooper found a key that fit. With a satisfying snick sound, the cell door opened.

Thornby stepped out. "Thank you. I am most grateful."

Bert pointed to the cell and said to the thug in suspenders, "Get in."

The bleeding man scooted in on his rump. Tombstone pushed the other injured smuggler in to join his fellow.

Bert rambled, "All right. Next thing is the telephones, I guess. Ace said to call ONI. Does she know it's possible? What if the lines aren't connected?"

The man in suspenders said, "Use the brown phone. It's connected to the main exchange." He glanced at his own bloody leg. "Use it to call a doctor."

Gooper's mustache bristled. "Don't yew wish."

Gooper clicked the cage closed.

The prisoner said, "I might bleed to death."

Gooper shrugged. "Cor. Now that'd be a pity."

Tombstone said, "Y'all ain't gonna die. Jes' keep quiet."

Bert peered toward the railway tunnel. "Where did Ace go?"

Tombstone spread his hands wide, palms up.

"Mebbe she ducked under the block of concrete afore it came down. Chasin' Braggs. Either she made it, or—" Tombstone stopped and looked like he'd swallowed a horny toad. He began again, "Well, let's say she made it, huh?"

"She made it!" Bert said fiercely.

Sam returned from the front door in a state of animation. "Sahibs. The man of very large size is coming to consciousness. I would like, if possible, some help. Also, the front entrance is sealed in a manner identical to the back."

There was a general rush to the front door and the recovering Futa. Futa sat up, and seemed to comprehend that the tommy guns pointed at him were significant.

"It is that I surrender," Futa said solemnly.

Sam studied some cranks and large gears in a wall

alcove. He said to Futa, "How long does it take to open the barriers?"

Futa shrugged massive shoulders. "If Futa does it, only eleven minutes." He touched his lower face, then examined the clotting blood on his fingertips. "Eleven minutes each, that is. There are two. One on this side and one on the side of the Old Slip Piers."

"Ah vote Old Slip Piers," Tombstone said.

Bert said, "Right. I'll see if the brown telephone connects."

"Call ONI," Ace said, and then sprinted after Braggs. She dove and rolled. Her crushed ribs sent spikes of pain, but she kept rolling. Her ears filled with the sound of scraping and rumbling as unstoppable forces crushed down lower and lower.

Ace rolled for yards, but still she wasn't in the clear. Ace's shoulder caught on the descending block! She could roll over and over no more. She stayed flat and wriggled like an electrocuted inchworm.

Her nose scraped stone, and then sensed free air. Her head was free. She yanked her feet out.

Boom! The huge block came to rest. Ace was uncrushed and whole, but something gripped her and held her immobile. After a moment, she realized that her coverall was pinched under the block at upper arm and thigh.

Ace stifled a sigh of relief as the stony echoes died

away. Braggs could be near, and she lay helpless. After a few moments, a rectangle of gloomy ambient city light appeared about ten feet further on.

Braggs's silhouette stepped through the rectangle and away. He did not bother to close the door. His footfalls receded, leaving only soft sounds of water lapping mingled with distant city noise.

Ace counted to ten after Braggs was lost to view, then she flexed her body. Sturdy canvas ripped reluctantly at knee and sleeve, but Ace won her freedom. Ace rose. Finding the dangling shreds bothersome, she finished the destruction of her sleeve. She ripped it loose and flung it off.

Focused and intent, Ace padded off to pursue Braggs. The bulky wooden door led to a forest of vertical timbers. The east river rippled and glistened past the posts. Weathered wooden planks provided both floor and ceiling.

Ace realized that she had emerged underneath the Old Slip Piers. The area was crowded and bustling in the day, but quiet now. Smells of fish and rotting fruit mingled uneasily in the air.

The arrangement was perfect for smugglers. Boats could dock at the Old Slip, but drop items down here for pickup. Whatever was dropped would disappear into the hideout. Outbound contraband could be placed on ships almost invisibly, perhaps even in daylight. Strategically draped nets blocked views from the river.

Ace searched the shadows for Braggs, moving catlike among the stained, salt-encrusted pilings. Traces of movement caught her eye, and she flitted to the left.

A dangling rope ladder.

Ace used it, ascending to the pier level. "I'm far behind already," she lamented to herself. "He ran, and I'm stuck to a snail's pace."

Cautiously, she poked her head up. Carts, bins, cranes, and winches limited her line of sight. She clambered up a crane, risking detection in the electric Manhattan glow. She stood on the corner of the cab and swept her head to absorb the panorama.

Ace reasoned that Braggs had two options. He was on the run. He would either hail a cab and disappear into New York, or stow away on a boat.

She scanned the pier. There were only two boats tied up to this particular slip, a rusty tramp steamer and a tug. The waterfront seemed desolate, but a fugitive lurked here, somewhere.

Ace closed her eyes and meditated on her sense of hearing, sorting out the sounds. Waves lapped softly. Buckles on ropes moved from the wind and clanged gently against their poles. A few seabirds called.

And someone was in trouble. Indistinct, faint yelps of distress emerged from the ambient sounds. Ace's golden eyes flashed open and zeroed in on the tramp steamer. Its engines chuffed, and it crept forward in the water.

For a frozen moment in time, Ace was a statue, poised like an eagle coasting on clement thermals. A moment later, nothing at all could be seen.

Chapter 30

"You know, a guy any less nervy than me would've blown that, when the ceiling block slid down. Good job, me!"

Tommy gun strapped to his back, Braggs climbed out of Smuggler's Crossroads into the legitimate world of commerce. He scanned around. The next pier over was the banana dock. No activity there right now, but when a boat landed, the bustle was intense as a horde of truck drivers tried to load simultaneously.

The dock he was standing on was shabbier and even cheaper. Because of the low rent, tramp steamers tied up here. Yes, there was one.

Braggs rubbed his chiseled jaw and winced. "That little fat man got me but good! I won't miss him in— hmm, where should I go? Baltimore, maybe. A nice, big city, Baltimore. Easy to get lost in the crowd. Piles of old money walking around, too."

Braggs jogged up the gangplank of the steamer. Straining, he dragged the planks of the ramp up onto the steamer's deck. Pausing to pant after the effort, he spotted a metallic gleam against the rust-streaked aft housing.

It was a machete, clipped to the wall within easy reach. Braggs claimed it. He whacked at the mooring ropes until they parted. The steamer drifted lazy inches away from the pier.

The fugitive spotted stairs down to a double row of tiny cabins. His even teeth grinned as he heard snoring. He checked all the doors, but there was only one occupied cabin.

He bonked the hilt of the machete on the sleeping man's skull, harder than necessary.

"Oww!" howled the man, a scrawny, bald, middle-aged sailor wearing baggy pants and no shirt. He tried to sit up.

"Shaddap," Braggs growled, pressing him down using the machete blade. "Listen to me, or you're dead. Dead! Got it?"

"Ow! Oh! Yeah, yeah, mister. What'ya want? All we got onboard is the tabbacy an' the wooden flutes!"

"I don't care about your stupid flutes. I want a taxi driver, and you're it. Start this boat and move it outta here. Clear? Be a good boy, now. I'm a bad boy, see? You'd scarcely believe how wonderfully awful I am."

Braggs grabbed him off the bed by the neck and shoved him out the door.

The sailor impacted the far side of the companionway. "Ow!"

"Faster. Get the engines going. I don't got all night." Braggs grinned, pleased at how ferocious his own voice sounded.

The whimpering sailor led the way to the engine room and fired up the fuel oil burners. Amid the dull roar of burning petroleum, the sailor said ingratiatingly, "I done what you asked, sir. It won't take long to build up a full head of steam. The water's still warm."

"Great. Now let's go steer." Braggs poked the

sweating sailor in the back, grinning at the resultant yelp.

Up on deck, Braggs scanned for people on the pier. No one. He slapped or poked the sailor from time to time, enjoying the way the bald man cringed and yipped at the abuse.

Braggs marched his victim up into the wheelhouse. Windows faced front, with doors wide open to starboard and port. The controls and the wheel were forward by the windows. "Just put it on full power," Braggs instructed.

"F-f-full? But there's a speed limit in the har—!"

"Shaddap!" Braggs punched him in the mouth.

After more whimpering, the sailor pulled two levers. New machine noises began. The ship sluggishly moved forward.

"There's a good egg." Braggs leered at him. "Now turn around."

The virile young man made a little circle gesture with his finger.

"Wh-what?"

"Turn around. Trust me."

Quaking, eyes wide, sweat streaming down his face, the sailor complied. Braggs crashed the hilt of the machete on his head. The sailor's limp body slithered to the floor.

"And that's why I'm unstoppable," crowed Braggs. "I wonder how much this ship is worth?"

He clapped the machete down on the front window sill and posed wide-legged at the helmsman's wheel. He gave the big wheel a lusty spin. The rudder dutifully responded and the ship yawed to port, much farther than Braggs intended. He cursed and reversed his spinning of the wheel, trying to avoid crashing into the next pier.

After the near-disaster, he treated the wheel with a lighter touch, and his course steadied. The steamer nosed out into the river.

"How did they find the warehouse?" Braggs muttered. "It was all going perfectly until then, except I didn't get my kiss from the scar-faced tomato. How did they find Smuggler's Crossroads? Sense of smell like a bloodhound?"

Movement caught his eye. He glanced out the wheelhouse door. Nothing.

But wait. He squinted at the deck. Wetness gleamed. The wet patches were oval, like footprints.

Braggs frowned, trying to make sense of it.

"No. Back here," said a voice behind him.

He spun around to face the opposite door. Like a golden ghost, Ace Carroway materialized. Her unarmed body seemed relaxed inside her tattered flight suit. Her lips compressed in distaste.

"You!" Braggs blurted.

"Well, hurry up. Your machete. Right there." Ace's mouth showed no mirth, but a note of dark humor colored her dry alto tones.

Braggs's face reddened. He lunged forward and seized the machete from the window sill. He faced Ace.

But she was gone from the doorway.

"Get back here, ya dizzy broad!" The more Braggs unraveled, the more his accents sank into the gutter. "Ugly spook!" He marched out of the wheelhouse, blade first.

As his hand broke the plane of the wheelhouse door, an airy whoosh puffed an eddy of air to Braggs's face. The half-seen blur was an oar swinging across the doorway. In the next instant, the oar smashed Braggs's wrist into the doorframe. Braggs howled in agony and the machete sailed off to clankety-clank down the deck astern.

Braggs whipped back inside, to clutch his injured wrist and groan until he could see more than pain stars. Cautiously, he poked his head barely out the door, surveying left, right, and even up. He saw only ship.

"Guess again," came a voice behind him.

Braggs whipped around. She was there. She stepped over the body of the bald sailor toward Braggs, eyes fixed on his center of mass.

He stared, mouth open in a grimace of horror. His tommy gun still swung on his back, the stock bumped his thigh, as if reminding him. He reached for the weapon, though only his left hand obeyed him.

"No," Ace said. With a lunge, she sank a fist in Bragg's gut. He doubled over. Ace struck again, knuckles curled for a precision strike. He felt a lancing pain in his shoulder and his left hand and arm dropped, sudden dead weights.

Something like a band of warm steel gripped his throat. The steely force pushed him backwards. His feet flew out from under him and he hit the deck flat on his back.

"Don't you recognize the game? It's called cat-and-mouse." Ace knocked his feeble right hand away and chopped his right shoulder with the heel of her hand.

Now, Braggs could feel neither arm. The pressure Ace exerted on his neck somehow blurred his vision. He gibbered inarticulately.

Ace's other hand peeled his suit jacket back and groped in his pocket. Braggs foamed at the mouth, his outrage almost overcoming his fear. But he was helpless.

Helpless!

Ace plucked his rat mask from his pocket. It was composed of straight ribs with painted fabric stretched over, so it would fold up small. Braggs had made it himself, and wore it with pride. She inspected it, then tossed it aside.

"It's confirmed. You're an overgrown mouse."

Braggs tried to kick his legs up to knock Ace off. She was buffeted, but applied more pressure to Bragg's neck. A new wave of dizziness washed over him.

As he fought for consciousness, he heard ice hard words.

"It's cat-and-mouse, Braggs. And guess what?"

But the blackness overwhelmed him.

"I'm the cat."

Chapter 31

Braggs struggled back to consciousness. He forced his eyes to focus. The wheelhouse and the ruddy New York skyglow resolved to clear images. He rolled over.

His heavy tommy gun flopped. He groped for it with arms that jangled with confused nerve impulses. But, though they complained, his arms obeyed him once again. His mashed right wrist and hand felt weak, but plenty strong enough to pull a tommy gun trigger. He staggered to his feet and looked out of the wheelhouse window.

The ship nestled cozily at the pier. Ropes moored them in place. The engines were silent.

"No. No, no, no!" he snarled through clenched teeth.

He heard a distant, soothing voice. "Don't try to get up, Avery. We'll get you to the hospital as soon as we can."

"Scarred witch!" Braggs's face pruned up in hatred and pain, and he lurched out of the wheelhouse.

"You're an angel sent from 'eaven, Miss Carroway," the bald sailor said. He and Ace were on deck amidships. He lay prone, propped up against a coil of rope. She knelt over him in a wet, torn flight suit.

Ace placed two fingers on Avery's neck to count his pulse. "I doubt that, but at least you'll have a whale of story to tell your mates."

"You!" Braggs growled, landing on the deck and stomping back toward them. He hefted his deadly tommy gun and leveled it at them. They were exposed. Easy targets.

Ace lifted her head. A vertical line appeared between her brows. "Braggs. Don't. It's over."

"Shut your yapper. It's not over. No wonder there's a price on your head; you're like a never-ending plague! You know what? Go on. Guess. Know what?"

Braggs leered madly. His rantings came in ragged gusts.

"I'm bad at guessing games. You're mad at me? You recover with astonishing swiftness after a carotid artery compression? You were bullied as a child?" During her speech, Ace slowly rocked to the balls of her feet and flexed her knees for action.

Avery the sailor choked out an inarticulate noise, but Ace didn't dare look at him. Her eyes locked on Braggs, especially on the muscle tension in his trigger finger.

"Oh, close your head, you ugly know-it-all! Here's what you don't know, Miss Scarface. You're still worth money dead. Full price alive, half price dead. I need the money, and I'm sick of you!" Flecks of spittle flew from his mouth as he spoke.

"Braggs. No." Ace winced in dread.

Braggs snarled, "Die!" and opened fire. His gun shuddered in his hands. Its muzzle flashed and it roared as it spat deadly points of lead. Ace dived sideways and rolled on the deck.

The bullets whizzed wild. After a short burst, Braggs staggered on his feet. His machine gun fell from his fingers with a clatter. He leaned sideways, then hit the deck. He moved no more. His unseeing eyes stared forward to where Ace rose from her crouch.

"What a sap," growled a voice. The rumpled trench coat and hat of Ironclad Case stepped into view from behind a capstan. A tendril of smoke rose from the business end of his steady .45 Colt.

On the corpse of Jeremy Braggs, a blotch of deep red at heart level spread sluggishly.

Ace grimaced at the sight, then raised her eyes to the rumpled figure. "Thank you, Ironclad. You saved our lives just now."

"I suppose so. I'm only here because of the phone call. Anyway, the good guys need to score a point once in a while."

The ONI agent pocketed his gun.

Pale Avery quavered, "Is it really over?"

Ironclad inserted a toothpick between his lips. "Over except for the paperwork. The paperwork never ends." He jerked a thumb toward the pier and said to Ace, "Here comes your crew."

The four associates slowed to a halt and lined up along the edge of the pier, eyes wide as they absorbed the scene on the deck.

Sam: "Lady Ace! Oh, I feel such joy!"

Tombstone: "Well, frizz my hair an' call me a sunrise! Ace is okay!"

Bert: "Ace, I see more of you than usual. I like it."

Gooper: "She's the baked bean! Braggs is brown bread, though.[3]"

Tombstone: "Whut? Talk English, you walrus."

---

[3] Cockney rhyming slang. Baked bean; the queen. Brown bread; dead.

CHAPTER 32

On opening night of the play, Bert showed up to the theater unaccompanied. He muttered something about Suzanne finding job applications more important than dates. But his surly attitude evaporated when the curtain rose. The associates and Ace soon lost themselves in the drama. Quack's identity seemed to disappear, and they saw only the questionably-sane Hamlet.

As the tragedy drew to a close, almost every character lay dead. The noble Norwegian prince Fortinbras solemnly ordered that the body of Hamlet be carried away with the pomp and ceremony due a fallen hero. Half the audience had tears streaming down their faces. The curtain descended.

The patrons erupted in thunderous applause, leaping to their feet and shouting, "Bravo!"

The curtain rose again, and the actors lined up and performed bows. Last to receive accolades was Boxnard Warburton Snana, known to Ace and her associates as Quack. He swept a deep bow.

A familiar, tall woman in a red dress stood at the edge of the stage and handed him a bouquet of flowers. His broad smile grew even broader. For a moment, however, a disturbing thought occurred, and Quack glanced up at the rigging.

But there was no one there.

YANKEES WIN

The Evening World.

"Circulation Books Open to All."

NEW YORK, FRIDAY, SEPTEMBER 23, 1921.

"Circulation Books Open to All."

Entered as Second-Class Matter
Post Office, New York, N. Y.

PRICE THREE CENTS

VOL. LXII. NO. 21,882—DAILY.

Copyright, 1921, by The Press Publishing
Co. (The New York World).

INDIANS GET TWO RUNS IN FOURTH INNING; RUTH FIRST TO SCORE FOR YANKEES

Hoyt Pitching Against Cove-
leak, Fans Three in First
—3,000 at Game.

By Bozeman Bulger.

BOX SCORE FOR SIX INNINGS.

CLEVELAND A.

	ab.	r.	h.	o.	a.	e.
Jamieson, lf	3	0	0	1	0	0
Evans, ss	3	0	1	2	3	0
Wood, rf	3	0	0	0	0	0
Smith, cf	3	0	0	2	0	0
Gardner, 3b	3	0	1	0	2	0
Sewell, ss	2	0	0	1	2	0
Johnston, 1b	3	1	1	5	0	0
O'Neill, c	2	0	0	4	1	0
Coveleskie, p	2	0	0	0	1	0
Totals	22	2	4	18	9	0

NEW YORK. A.

	ab.	r.	h.	o.	a.	e.
Fewster, lf	3	0	0	0	0	0
Peckinpaugh, ss	3	0	1	3	1	0
Ruth, rf	2	1	1	1	0	0
Meusel, cf	2	0	0	1	0	0
Pipp, 1b	2	0	0	4	0	0
Ward, 2b	2	0	1	2	3	0
McNally, 3b	2	0	0	0	2	0
Schang, c	2	0	0	4	0	0
Hoyt, p	2	0	0	0	1	0

Evening World Racing Chart

AQUEDUCT, N. Y., SEPT. 23.—WEATHER CLEAR. TRACK GOOD.

715

716

717

RESULT

	First	Second	Third
	1	2	3

TWO PLUCKY YOUNG BOYS CARRYING $10,700 PAYROLL FOIL BANDIT PISTOL IN HAND

With Revolver Pointed in His
Face, Bank Messenger Blows
Whistle Until Hold-Up Men
Flee Near Broadway.

**Suspect Captured on Roof
After Highwayman is
Chased Through Building in
University Place.**

Two plucky bank messengers, both
of them young boys and one with the
nerve to blow a police whistle with a
hold-up man's revolver thrust in his
face, will obtain to-day...

PIANIST AND ACE PILOT
ONE AND THE SAME

CHEMIST RESCUED
DEAD IN RAID
TWO GANG MEMBERS

MISS MILDRED HANAN SHOT FROM AMBUSH BY WOMAN WHO THEN ENDS OWN LIFE

Mrs. Grace Lawes Trails Victim on Auto Trip and Fires as She and Escort Leave Brooklyn House—Note Blames "Too Much High Life"

Miss Mildred E. Hanan, devoted wife of Dr. Jerome Wagner, and
daughter of Alfred P. Hanan, shoe millionaire and his divorced wife, Mrs.
Clara W. Hanan, was shot and fatally hurt in Schermerhorn Street,
Brooklyn, at 1 o'clock this morning. Mrs. Grace Lawes of San Francisco
shot Miss Hanan and then shot and killed herself.

NOTES

At this point in The Adventures of Ace Carroway, the brew of ingredients for the Ace Carroway saga are in place: five associates, a detective agency with Mrs. Figgins, facial scars, and a growing reputation. I'm looking forward to firing up the heat under this cauldron. Wait 'til you see what bubbles up.

I would be remiss if I did not mention that, although "carotid artery compression" would act physiologically approximately as I describe, in the real world, recovery is not certain. The artery can easily stay collapsed. To put it mildly, this would be very bad, so please tag this concept with a huge stamp that says "Do not try this at home!"

The swashbuckling character Zorro was created in 1919 by pulp fiction writer Johnston McCulley. The success of the 1920 film "The Mark of Zorro" starring Douglas Fairbanks stimulated McCulley to write more tales of Zorro, which he did for forty years. Zorro is one of the first fictional heroes with a secret identity, requiring him to wear a mask. The masked hero concept has enjoyed great popularity.

The banana docks and Old Slip Piers are real historical places. It's hard to say if Smuggler's Crossroads was real. There is no mention of such a place in the historical record. But, if it were real, wouldn't they want to keep it secret?

Thank you for reading! I'll see you again shortly, when Ace investigates an unnerving growl sound that accompanies mayhem, kidnapping, and death.

ABOUT THE AUTHOR

Wyoming native Guy Worthey traded spurs and lassos for telescopes and computers when he decided to pursue astrophysics. Whenever he temporarily escapes the gravitational pull of stars and galaxies, he writes fiction, now in the slightly less rectangular state of Washington. He plays jazz bass and happily stretches genre boundaries to find common musical ground with his classical violinist wife Diane. A beacon of inclusivity in a fractured world, he likes both cats and dogs. Creamed eggs on toast is the earthy name of his favorite food, but once in a while he samples the celestial delights of chocolate.

ACKNOWLEDGMENTS

Thanks to my readers, especially my early readers that get versions as riddled with holes as that nasal-voiced fellow in Smuggler's Crossroads. Thanks to Mikey Brooks and Brian Gagnon for their artistic pizzazz. Thanks and love to my wonderful family.

THE ADVENTURES OF ACE CARROWAY

Book 1
ACE CARROWAY AND THE GREAT WAR

Book 2
ACE CARROWAY AROUND THE WORLD

Book 3
ACE CARROWAY AND THE HANDSOME DEVIL

Book 4
ACE CARROWAY AND THE GROWLING DEATH

Book 5
ACE CARROWAY AND THE MIDNIGHT SCREAM

Book 6
ACE CARROWAY AND THE DEADLY VIOLIN

Book 7
ACE CARROWAY AND THE GHOST LINER

Book 8
ACE CARROWAY AND THE BLIND PANIC

guyworthey.net